To my dear ⟨…⟩ ⟨…⟩ ⟨…⟩ ⟨…⟩ ⟨…⟩ ⟨…⟩ie
"A joy forever ⟨…⟩

Hub City Christmas

Hub City Christmas

Spartanburg Writers Trim the Literary Tree

editors,

 Betsy Wakefield Teter & John Lane

Holocene 1997

ISBN 0-9638731-4-8
First edition, Christmas 1997

Cover & book design by Mark Olencki
Historic illustrations by Dover Art Services
Cover photograph of Bonhaven, located near downtown
  Spartanburg, courtesy of Cleveland family archives
Special thanks to Scott Gould for helping to select the essays
Printed & bound by Thomson-Shore, Inc. in Dexter, Michigan

Holocene Publishing
Post Office Box 8421
Spartanburg, South Carolina 29305
(864) 597-0740 • fax (864) 597-4549
e-mail: *laneje@wofford.edu*

Table of Contents

Preface

When the *Hub City Anthology* came out in April of '96 we were already thinking about this book. We saw the chance to gather together a chorus of Spartanburg voices celebrating the Christmas season. We circulated a call for manuscripts—1,000-word personal stories about Christmas in Spartanburg—placed a notice in the local paper, and waited. As we had done with *Hub City Anthology*, we were creating something from nothing. We trusted the process. We had a suspicion the response would not be silence. We received almost sixty submissions and asked a writer from outside the community to help us select the ones that would work best together as an anthology. Our reader was impressed with the quality and variety.

It's said every snowflake is a little different, and stories in a community are much like snowflakes: male and female stories, black and white, Jewish and Christian, young and old, stories full of sorrow and joy. The truth of our diverse visions became very obvious when the final selection was made, and thirty-two personal stories about Spartanburg Christmas, past and present, were edited, placed in order, typeset, and sent to the printer. Who would have guessed that a call for submissions for this anthology in November would have brought stories from twenty-five different zip codes?

It doesn't snow much in the Hub City, but this season it's snowing stories. Buy this book as a gift, but here are several other suggestions: buy this book for yourself. Just before Christmas, when everyone else's presents are finally wrapped, get a cup of mulled cider and sit somewhere in a soft chair. Open this book at random and read, sipping as you go—both good cider and good writing.

—Betsy Wakefield Teter & John Lane

SWEETNESS AND LIGHT
By Carlin Morrison

Sweetness and light, black and white, Sodom and Gomorrah, sugar and spice, nuts and bolts. My mother has a mental filing system, a plethora of three-word clichéd expressions with which she can classify any personality, situation, event, philosophy, or emotion. Christmas is always sweetness and light.

I'm not quite sure how she arrived at this summation of the holiday. I guess because, despite her often fierce sense of realism, my mother is ultimately an optimist. Christmas is sweetness simply because the family, scattered across the Carolinas, comes together for twenty-four hours. Twenty-four hours of kisses and hugs, snacks, insincere fawning over deviled eggs and children, mountains of presents, fights over the TV remote, ten desserts, three versions of sweet potatoes, cranky infants and morose teenagers, and at least one pleading appeal of "can't we all get along" that all translate into bliss

11

for my mother.

Christmas is light for the same reason. But to my mother, and much of the rest of the South, Christmas is quite literally "lights." A festival of garishness. An art form with the house and front yard as a canvas. A hootin', hollerin' good time for Duke Power. I've noticed that over the past ten years or so, light displays have become more intricate and expansive, creeping like kudzu from the tree in the living room to front porches, eaves, chimneys, bushes, lamp posts, and mail boxes. Artificial, multi-colored beacons shine forth, summoning families to load the kids up and drive by before the midnight church service. Two years ago, in my mother's home of Burlington, North Carolina, we drove to the edge of Alamance County where a small farm is annually transformed into a two-thousand-watt tourist attraction. Last holiday season, the family descended on my brother in Charlotte, and he dutifully herded us into the minivan to see the luminous festival at Heritage USA, proving to me, at least, that the nameless spirit that inspired Tammy Faye's make-up had survived that scandal with renewed strength. And this Christmas . . . this Christmas it was my turn.

Everyone was coming to Spartanburg, the first holiday I'd hosted in my young life. So many things to think about: Where could my stepfather sneak off to smoke a cigarette without fear of incrimination? How could I let "The Little Mermaid" play twenty-two times on the big-screen TV without my husband killing a child? How was I going to squeeze sixteen settings of inherited Christmas china on the poker/dining room table and two card tables? And most importantly, where was there a truly retina-damaging light display in Spartanburg? The other problems surely had solutions, but what about this last question? It loomed over my head as I baked every drop of moisture out of the turkey, crept into my dreams during my three-hour stints of sleep, made me break into a cold sweat as we strung lights on our tree. Finally it hit me, an idea that lit up in my head like a hundred-foot string of super-brite indoor/outdoor lights. I would take the family on a tour of lights, a caravan weaving its way through the city past an array of individually strung miracles.

13

Christmas dinner ran on a par with previous years: my stepfather was able to covertly smoke a half a pack of cigarettes, my husband not only let all the children live, but hummed "Under the Sea" until New Year's and, though we looked as if our elbows had been glued to our rib cages while we ate, all the Christmas china sat pretentiously displayed on the makeshift tables. But I fidgeted through the motions, an anxious daughter waiting to give her mother a present she had picked out all by herself. I threw slabs of Lane cake and Miracle pie in front of people, put ice cubes in the coffee so they'd drink it more quickly, snatched dolls out of one hand and thrust unopened presents in the other of my confused nieces, shoved old and young alike toward the door like I was the leader of a cattle drive; they had to see the montage of Spartanburg's light fantastic.

I made the executive decision to take my brother's minivan so that everyone could ride together. I wouldn't be denied one "ooh" or "aah." Not enough room? So what if Great Nannie had to sit where groceries usually do? Finally, however, the grunts, groans, bruised knees, and smarting funny bones brought me back to my senses. We would take two cars, I conceded, but only two.

My plan dictated that we should start in Converse Heights, its landscaped trees and manicured lawns a breeding ground for meticulous light-art perfection. We drifted on the bath of light spilled out from the luminaire-lined streets, past architectural exactness enunciated with crisp white lights. Deep green garlands interwoven with small bulbs and punctuated with rich garnet bows adorned every doorway, post, and window. This was a treat for my mother's eyes, I smiled, self-satisfied; decorations applied with Cartier taste and a slide rule.

"On to Hampton Heights," I declared to my husband. My coup de grâce. Refurbished Victorians done up in antiquated style. My mother would surely gasp aloud, "Currier & Ives," as we drove past life-sized incarnations of the ceramic Victorian village that sat on her coffee table for the past twenty-some-odd years.

Luminous, the god of crushed blinker bulbs and working light strands, was obviously with me, for as we drove past the glowing gazebo and historical plaque, we met a horse-drawn carriage carrying a family sunk deep in tartan wool blankets. Along the sidewalk other families, pointing and nudging, followed a tour guide, white plumes puffing from her mouth. I didn't need to see any more; I had given my mother a scene from "A Christmas Carol." How good did Heritage look now? I turned around in the car seat, steadying myself for my mother's mouthed kudos through the windshield. But she was . . . she was nodding at me. Mouthing "PRETTY." I had seen that nod before. It was the "we'll see" nod that infuriated countless numbers of children throughout history. It was the noncommittal nod, the "I've not decided" nod. Surely she was impressed! Surely she hadn't seen Christmas card displays like this at a farm in Alamance County!

I turned back around, dejected, defeated and muttered, "Let's go home." Where had I gone wrong? Why did my family, with their fire-hazard, ten-plugs-in-one-outlet trees, and their blinking bushes, and their plastic red-tipped window candles, why did they have the gall to look bored? I had shown them the Michelangelo's Pieta of decorative lights, and . . . and I don't live in the Pieta of families, my brain said. I've seen the Pieta; the

15

hem of Mary's garment is carved so thinly, so delicately, that the marble is translucent. My family is a rambling, boisterous mass of barely contained chaos and enthusiasm. Translucent marble wouldn't stand a chimeless chance. It is said that Michelangelo tried to destroy the work; an apprentice pulled him off, the only real damage done to Mary's left-hand little finger. My nieces could have taken that finger off with two good whacks.

"Take the back way home," I told my husband. "The scenic route."

We drove past trees haphazardly wrapped with 1970s-style large-bulb, multi-hued lights, chips missing out of the enamel. To the right was a yard with a "Santa Stops Here" sign and a blinking-nosed Rudolph to greet him. To the left, the bushes were wrapped in what looked like a child's Jacob's Ladder of uncoordinated blinking lights. Further down the street was a house with every plane and line traced drunkenly with icicle lights and cherry-red bows. The light from the strands showed a roughly carved nativity scene with the baby Jesus' halo in a chasing blink pattern. A block down, a yard housed a half-lit Santa mechanically waving and bowing from the waist like some sort of electro-dynamic yuletide machine digging a well or drilling for oil. Another house looked like the resident had opened up the window and thrown forty stands of lights on the bushes outside. And yet another, farther down the block, had ornaments and lights that appeared as if they had been found in an archaeologist's excavation, since he has left his decorations out year-round at least as long as I've lived in Spartanburg.

The back street had been a dizzying array of color, overdone fervor, and overt, albeit crookedly strung, cheer. I again turned in my seat to see my mother, herself turned to her grandchildren in the backseat, laughingly pointing out reindeer sitting askew on the last roof. I turned back around, thinking of the three-word clichés she could be saying: Dasher and Dancer or Prancer and Vixen. They wouldn't sum up any particular "ism" or emotional state, but for the time, they would do. 🎄

17

2

CHRISTMAS AT CROFT

By Kirk Neely

When I was two years old my parents were asked to leave First Baptist Church. This had nothing to do with my being in the terrible two-year-old stage of childhood development. Mom and Dad were asked to go to Camp Croft, an abandoned military camp outside the Spartanburg city limits used by the United States Army to train soldiers during World War II. There were several vacant military chapels remaining at Camp Croft. One of them had been purchased by First Baptist Church as a mission site. Mom and Dad were sent to start the mission. My dad, who still runs a lumberyard as his regular work, has always been a devoted churchman. At Camp Croft he did almost everything— repairing the building, leading the singing, serving as deacon chairman, sometimes preaching, and praying without ceasing.

Christmas at Croft was always a happy time. One of the high points was the Sunday night in December that we presented our Christmas pageant. Every young person in our church took part in the Christmas pageant. I was always a shepherd. Any boy who did not have one of the major parts, Joseph or a Wise Man, was automatically relegated to the role of shepherd. Any girl who did not have a major part, Mary or the Archangel, had to be an angel in the heavenly host.

A shepherd did not need much equipment. Shepherds went barefooted. They wore towels draped and secured on their heads with old neckties, and they wore their fathers' bathrobes. My dad did not have a bathrobe. I had to wear my mother's red quilted bathrobe.

A shepherd also had to have a staff. At Croft we tried several kinds over the years. There were the cardboard shepherd's crooks that did well until they got wet, soggy, and floppy. There were the shepherd's crooks made from a broom handle and a bent coat hanger. These turned out to be lethal weapons. Finally, there were the top-of-the-line shepherd's crooks that my dad cut out of quarter-inch plywood at the lumberyard. When we gathered in the foyer of the church with those plywood shepherd's crooks, the clacking together sounded as if we were having a sword fight.

I was always a shepherd until one year Gregory was sick with the flu. Gregory was always Joseph, and Jenny was always Mary. Gregory was sweet on Jenny, but Jenny seemed unmoved by his attention. On Wednesday night before the Christmas pageant, the pastor's wife, who was always the director, told me that Gregory was ill. I would have to be Joseph.

This called for several major revisions. First of all, my mother's bathrobe would no longer do. I was told that I would wear the pastor's bathrobe, which looked like Joseph's coat of many colors must have looked. We rolled up the sleeves and cinched the belt tight. The robe was bloused above the belt so the back wouldn't drag across the floor. I was still allowed to go barefooted, but I did have to have a different towel. White was too plain for Joseph. The one I wore was striped and was tied on with one of the pastor's gaudy cast-off ties.

The biggest problem I had was that I had to stand close to Jenny. At that time in my life, I felt really uncomfortable around any girl. Jenny was the prettiest girl in the church. She was a year older than I was, and it showed. To stand close to Jenny would have been hard in any circumstance, but to stand close to Jenny wearing the pastor's bathrobe was almost more than I could take.

We practiced the pageant on Wednesday night. Several men in the church worked on the spotlights that were to be focused on the stage. Jenny and I walked down the aisle and placed a Betsy-Wetsy doll in a manger made from scrap lum-

21

ber. Beverly, the Archangel, stood in the baptistery window above the scene and told about good tidings of great joy. The shepherds came down the aisle. The heavenly host sang to them, and the wise men walked forward and presented their gifts. There was a cigar box wrapped in gold Christmas paper, a Witch Hazel bottle wrapped in tin foil, and an Old Spice aftershave bottle. We had rehearsed well. We were ready.

On Saturday before the Christmas pageant, Gregory was well. He said, "Kirk, please let me be Joseph. I already know how to do it, and I can do it better than you." I said, "No, I have practiced and I think I can do it." Gregory was a persuasive fellow. When I wouldn't budge, he moved to one of the wise men and talked him into being a shepherd. At least Gregory could be a wise man.

The night of the pageant came. Our cue was to walk down the aisle when certain carols were played on the piano. Jenny and I, as Mary and Joseph, would go into the sanctuary when we heard "O Little Town of Bethlehem." We stood in the foyer with wise men and shepherds clacking those plywood staffs together in spite of themselves. Jenny cracked the door open and peeked inside at the assembled worshipers. She said with alarm, "Ya'll, there are people in there." She excused herself to go to the bathroom, leaving me holding the doll.

While she was gone, the piano started playing "O Little Town of Bethlehem." I stood there with a Betsy-Wetsy doll, not knowing what to do. By the second verse, which was played a little louder, Jenny was back, and we walked down the aisle together. When she put baby Jesus, the Betsy-Wetsy doll, down in the manger, it issued forth a cry that sounded like a mad cat. I didn't remember the doll crying during rehearsal. I got tickled and struggled desperately not to giggle out loud.

As I stood there in the pastor's bathrobe next to Jenny with the spotlights glaring, I became aware that it was very hot. In those days I wore a flat-top haircut. I used a product known as Butch Hair Wax on my flat-top to make it stand up straight. Between the spotlights with the towel tied on my head, trying to control the giggles, standing next to Jenny, wearing the pastor's bathrobe, my hair wax started to melt. I could feel it oozing down my forehead. I used the sleeve of the pastor's bathrobe to wipe it away from my eyes.

23

The shepherds came down the aisle and took their places with crooks rattling. Beverly, the Archangel, came into the baptistery. Beverly wore braces. When the spotlight hit those braces it really did look as if the glory of the Lord was shining all round about her. Then the heavenly host came through the side door. The problem was that they had practiced without their wings. Their wings were wider than the door. The first angel in got stuck. A helpful mother turned each angel sideways and sent them in one at a time.

Now it was time for the wise men to come and present gifts to the baby Jesus. They made their way down the aisle. The first brought the cigar box wrapped in gold paper. The second one came with the Old Spice aftershave bottle. Gregory was last. I think he must have been about halfway down the aisle when he realized that he had forgotten to bring a gift. In his last-minute rush to get one of the main parts, he left out one of the most important things. As I wiped away the Butch Hair Wax from my forehead with the sleeve of the pastor's bathrobe, I saw Gregory hike up his own bathrobe and reach in his pocket.

The wise men got to the front of the church. The cigar box wrapped in gold paper was laid by the manger. The Old Spice Aftershave bottle was carefully put in place. Finally Gregory placed his gift at the feet of baby Jesus, a Duncan Spinner Yo-Yo.

I have often thought about that Christmas pageant at Croft. It certainly was different from the slick, professional ones that are presented in places like the Crystal Cathedral or even in the large, sophisticated churches I have served since Croft. But in some ways, that Christmas pageant at Croft is more like the first Christmas than any of the others could ever be. The people in that first Christmas pageant in Bethlehem so long ago were so much like us. There was a young woman, probably a teenager, about to have her first baby in a stable. There was a carpenter who, like the character Prissy in "Gone With the Wind," didn't know a thing about birthing babies. The shepherds, the blue-collar workers of their day, were just minding their own business when they were overcome with fear, wondering what on earth, and what in heaven, was happening. And there were the wise men, who hitched their caravan to a star, bringing gifts as precious to them as a Duncan Yo-Yo is to a young boy.

In the Christmas pageant at Croft, we always concluded the service by singing "Away in a Manger." There is a line in that carol that says, "The Little Lord Jesus, no crying he makes," but I'll bet he did. Just as surely as that Betsy-Wetsy doll cried, I'll bet the baby Jesus cried. I do too. I laugh, and I cry every time I remember Christmas at Croft.

25

OVERBROOK CIRCLE
By Marsha Poliakoff

One December morning in Spartanburg some thirty years ago, a loud knock on the open door brought me to the porch where two parallel figures were waiting: a tall man and a huge tree, a Christmas tree, both unexpected. My two sons, Bobby and Mike, age five and six, scurried around me and flung the door all the way open. The man explained that the Christmas tree was his gift for work my husband, an attorney, had done for him. Smiling broadly, he asked, "Where do you want it?"

Should I tell him that we're Jewish and never had a tree, and wouldn't know what to do with one? If I turned him away with his tree, the boys would be terribly disappointed, the man wouldn't understand, and his wonderful smile would fade quickly.

As a Jewish family, we celebrated Chanukah, but Christmas was no stranger to us. Like everyone around us, we were caught up in its sparkling web. The man lifted the tree over the threshold and stood it in the hall. He glanced into the living room and said he knew exactly where to put it. He set the tree in its container in the middle of the room and its uppermost branch brushed the ceiling and bent in submission. My husband's client renewed his smile, wished us a Merry Christmas, then jumped into his red pick-up truck and was gone.

"It sure is big. If it grows, it'll go right through your ceiling!" The voice had a sweet ring like that of a boy soprano. It belonged to Buster, the neighbor's nine-year-old boy. I hadn't seen him come in.

28

He stood back, admiring the tree that almost filled the room. "Let's get your ornaments," he said. His cherubic apple-cheeks framed his laughing smile, his eyes bright with expectation. I told him that this was our first tree, and we didn't have ornaments.

He pondered for a moment. "We can put toys on it . . . and presents."

The boys chimed in, "Let's do it, Mommy! Can we? Please!"

I popped some corn and strung it over the tree, and my sons excitedly rounded up their miniature racing cars and balsam wood airplanes. Buster tied their toys to the sprays of green needles, while the boys, trying to help, were clumsily working inept fingers and bumping into each other. They watched with bated breath, as each branch wavered in accepting or refusing its burden. Sometimes the twig snapped and formed a right angle, while the toy hung in place. Then Bobby and Mike screamed with delight. It was a match between determination and gravity, and determination was winning. To my amazement, the tree was beginning to look quite festive. I turned to gather my reward of smiles, but Buster was not smiling.

"We don't have a tree. My mother hasn't had time to buy one."

I told him that he could visit ours whenever he wanted, but I worried that he and my sons, if they got into a hassle, would be unequally matched. Buster was large and burly, and three years older than my eldest. Buster was a latchkey child. His father had passed away that year, and his mother had to work. So far, he had been pleasant and gentle, and his voice was always cheerful. He came every day, and would move and adjust the hanging toys from branch to branch, tongue over lip, in rapt concentration.

Later that week, my sons did not appear at suppertime. I looked for them at the vacant lot, where they usually played ball. No one was there. Searching up and down Overbrook's streets, I spotted my two boys and Buster, pushing and dragging a large fir tree up the hill. I met them as they struggled with their burden. Green fir needles stuck to the perspiration on their foreheads from

29

under their red, woolen caps, and bits and pieces of greenery studded their jackets and jeans. I asked how they had gotten the tree, and Buster, breathless from dragging his heavy prize uphill, said in spurts, that he had saved his lunch money and had smashed open his glass dog bank . . . and found a wonderful deal on this tree . . . "cause it's only a little bit broken."

Suddenly, a voice split the air like a buzzsaw. It came from the stoop of the house next to ours. "Buster, you little . . . What in the devil are you dragging?" It was Buster's mother, Bert, tall and stout, hands on her ample hips.

"It's a Christmas tree, and I got a good deal on it."

"It's garbage!" she yelled.

Bert was from a big Northern city, and her forthcoming manner and unvarnished honesty were disarming. "Where did you get the money?" she demanded.

He explained that he had been saving lunch money for a bicycle, but changed his mind and bought the tree.

"So you're starving yourself, and you're thin as a rail."

Buster was not at all thin. Compared to my boys, he was immense. But who can argue with a protective mother?

"Get in this house right now. Your supper is on the table."

"I don't want it. I want to eat with Bobby and Mike."

Bert's eyes were reddening, and she compressed her in-drawn lips. "I don't know what to do with him. Ever since his father died, he won't eat."

"Let him eat with us," Bobby urged.

Buster had dinner with us that evening and almost every evening after that. I invited Bert, but she always declined, saying she needed to get her housework done.

On Christmas day, Buster brought me a package, elegantly wrapped, bearing the gold seal of the best emporium in Spartanburg, the Aug. W. Smith Company.

"It's from me and my mom," he said in his angelic voice.

31

I opened the wrappings and found a beautiful, blue glass candy jar with a note from Bert. It said, "With appreciation for looking after Buster."

The years passed and we moved away. The boys grew up, and Buster got married, and later Bert had kidney failure and died. I went to her funeral, and saw Buster, whom I hadn't seen in years, and he had grown very tall and broad. Obviously, his mother's worries about his becoming "thin as a rail" were totally unfounded. We all hugged and wept, and he said he would never forget us. His voice, now deeper, still had its sweetness. For a moment, it felt like we were back on Overbrook Circle.

I learned some time later that Buster, at the height of his young manhood, passed away. He'd had an illness, some form of diabetes, and I heard that his wife had cared for him devotedly through-out. Who deserved the gift, the blue glass candy jar, more than the young woman who cared for him? Bert's note was in my jewelry box where I had saved it all these years. I slipped it inside the candy jar, which I wrapped and delivered. I hope she found the note, "With appreciation for looking after Buster."

Christmas at Cedar Grove
Pre-Civil War

"At the end of one table, in front of Colonel Moore, was a pig roasted whole, with an apple in his mouth; at the other end, before Miss Rebecca, stood a mammoth turkey. Farther down, about midway at one side, a fine boiled ham, some six or seven years cured; across from it stood an immense chicken pastry; and grouped around were dishes of the vegetable order—rice, potatoes (sweet and Irish). Dried fruit, canned tomatoes, corn, etc.; eggs dressed in different ways; pickles, jellies, catsups, sauces, etc."

—From the book, "Thirty Four Years: An American Story of Southern Life," by Celina E. Means, published by Claxton, Remsen & Haffelfinger (1878).

33

DADDY'S CHRISTMAS DRAMA
By Evelyn Brock Waldrop

The first Christmas I remember was my fourth, in 1920, but the tree-lighting ritual at our house must have begun years earlier. It had accumulated the aura of a tradition too sacred to question, and it remained virtually unchanged throughout my Spartanburg childhood.

35

We lived on West Main Street, in a huge century-old white frame house that stood behind magnolia trees far back from the narrow cobblestone street. An ornate arch separated our broad front hall from the back hall and stairway.

The arch was hidden during the winters. Daddy had filled the space with a removable beaver-board wall. Its function was to keep the front rooms free from the drafts that seeped in from the back door. Without central heating, every BTU of warmth from coal heaters and fireplace logs had to be cherished.

To hide the unsightly partition and its narrow door, Mamma had hung a pleated green plush curtain. It was in front of the curtain that our tall Christmas tree was placed.

Decorating our tree was an exciting semi-public event that our cousins and neighbors seldom missed. Its scenario had been created by Daddy, whose benevolent authority as producer, director, and star were unquestioned.

For the noisy prelude, we children were cast as extras as well as audience. We were allowed to adorn the lower branches with glass ornaments, paper chains, garlands of tinsel, and cascades of aluminum icicles. Then, as we sat squirming on the rug, Daddy would mount his sturdy step ladder, explaining that it was off-limits to everyone else, and decorate the high branches, ending with a lopsided tinsel star at the top. This was Act One.

The drama intensified as he attached to the branch tips dozens of tin spring-clip candle holders, each with its slim wax candle. The strategic placement of each candle was an exact science which only Daddy understood.

As my sisters relayed clips and candles up to Daddy, he rewarded us with his annual sermon on fire hazards, the tinder-box nature of evergreens, and all the reasons why nobody, *nobody*, NOBODY was ever to light any of the candles unless he and Mamma were present and prepared.

Everybody understood that "prepared" fore-told yet another ritual. Its props consisted of a garden hose attached to the bathtub faucet off the back hall, and extended through a hole high in the partition. As the trusty step ladder waited, ready for the star of the production to mount if needed, Mamma would be stationed in the back hall, ready to rush to the tub and turn on the faucet at Daddy's signal. The rules were rehearsed until even we toddlers understood their importance.

On selected evenings during Christmas week, the growing audiences of kids sat spellbound while Daddy climbed up and slowly lighted each candle, maintaining his priestly authority. Sighs of relief, like small amens from us acolytes, punctuated the ceremony as each candle flame was steadied and declared acceptable. Then, balancing himself carefully, Daddy grasped the nozzle of the hose, first making sure Mamma was at her place.

The reward of this elaborate ritual was about ten minutes of absolute magic. Room lights were turned off to allow the candles to glow like small flickering stars, while Mamma's clear soprano led us in a carol sing.

All too soon for us, Daddy slowly blew out the candles and the overhead lights went on. As Daddy folded the ladder and rolled up the hose, the aromas of wax and warm cedar mingled with the welcome smell of cookies and cocoa Mamma served, perhaps as a thank offering. Her loved ones had again been kept safe and happy by the grace of God and the diligence of Daddy. The candlelight, the fragrances, the music, and the sequences of quiet reverence and noisy celebration are etched in my memory forever.

Mamma had cautioned us not to brag, but I remember feeling smugly superior to my playmates throughout these annual evidences of paternal protectiveness. I was sure no other daddy was so smart and willing to do so much to create those brief moments of perilous pleasure.

As electric tree lights became affordable, everyone's holidays became safer. But Christmas trees never again have seemed as exciting as those with candles licking their tiny flames among the ornaments and volatile needles.

And no house since has seemed as steeped in Christmas as the rambling frame house on West Main. It kept its roof held high years after the surrounding houses were bulldozed to make room for used car lots and fast food drive-ins.

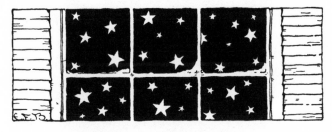

Christmas near Pauline
1861

"December 25: Christmas has come once more and
has gone again. But few guns have been fired in honer of
Christmas & not much sign of merriment. Santa Claus did not
pay us his accomstomed visit last night. Some think the good
old man has been taken prisner by the Yankeys & his cargo
of toys confisticated."

—*From "Piedmont Farmer: The Journals of David Golightly
Harris 1855-1879," edited by Philip N. Racine.*

39

OF SANTA AND BABY JESUS
By Cooper Smith

Spartanburg was just a haze in our heads then, somewhere on past Gaffney, known only by a voice, Farmer Gray, and country music over a static-filled, battery radio. We little ones, sleeping four thick on a straw tick, at 5:30 sharp would hear Daddy's booming voice, "It's time to get up!" Hitting the ice-cold floor, we'd make a fire in the fireplace and kitchen stove to Roy Acuff's "Way Deep in the Hills" or Little Jimmy Dickens' "Sleeping at the Foot of the Bed" over WSPA.

It was a time and place of the happiest, richest poverty you could ever know. Around 1939 or 1940 and about thirty-nine or forty miles north of Spartanburg deep in the woods at the end of a dirt road on the banks of Kings Creek in a clearing three miles from Kings Mountain Battleground, a house stood on rock pillars with cotton and corn fields on either side and new grounds toward the creek. A barn, a chicken house, an outhouse, a hog pen, a corn crib, each with its own path, were in the clearing also. A well-worn path led to the spring, three paths and two wagon roads to the creek, and all around, trees: poplars, oaks, maples, dogwoods, pines, cedars, and hollies, some designating places and directions—the maple in Russell field, the black gum by the mud hole.

This was the place of my first nine Christmases. Although remote, it was part of an enveloping community populated by people who believed their lot was to work hard, look after their own, support Joe Louis and trust God and Franklin D. Roosevelt. No one would have thought to question this credo. The Depression was upon us and so was discipline.

Of course, all was not sinless. There was some moonshining, miscegenation, and an occasional rumor or fact of a single girl pregnant; and the big boys would curse the mules when Daddy wasn't around. But the two-parent families, the strict teachings at the Presbyterian church and the Rosenwald school house, and the credo of work, care, and trust held sway, and so got us from Christmas to Christmas. Like the other families in the community of Hopewell, we fourteen children and Momma and Daddy fully bought the lore of Christmas.

But the pristine and delirious joy, the delicious wonder of it were more with us little ones than with our older brothers and sisters. We soaked up the baby Jesus and Santa Claus stories like cotton absorbing gasoline. Putting those stories into our innocent and fanciful minds in this setting of hot summers, hard winters and jet-black, star-sprinkled nights—in this setting of caring and sanctioning adults who made you sit up and look straight ahead in church—putting these stories in our minds in this environment was either an exceedingly good or very cruel thing to do. There is no way it could have *not* mattered, no way we could have resisted, shaken off those stories or that culture. There was no distinction, no counter to them. They made an immediate, deep, and enduring difference in us.

But a time did come when we wanted to be rid of that place, the watchful community . . . and the baby Jesus story. It was after going to Gaffney on the train with my sister at age seven and to Charlotte with Daddy at eight that I first started wanting to get out of the woods, away from those caring and correcting eyes. And yes, in spite of, or maybe because of, Sunday School, I'd just as soon have forgotten that baby Jesus stuff too.

But I was prepared to fight, and did, to keep Santa. I hit the dirt with my little foul-mouth cousin when he said, "Santa Claus is ya momma and daddy." When I discovered the chimney was too small for Santa, I told myself he came through the door. And one Christmas morning when I saw by my pile of gifts a note, "To Cooper from Santa,"

43

I happily announced, "Santa Claus writes just like Lean," Evangeline, my oldest sister. I turned mule tracks to reindeer hooves, and knew Santa came over the tree tops when the road was covered smoother with snow. The better the arguments against Santa, the more imaginative and elaborate were my explanations for him.

Why this need to keep Santa and jettison Jesus? It must have been because Santa made us "good," worthy through work, approved by our parents; made us feel not only happy, but proud—at least for a short time—and he gave immediate, concrete rewards. But the baby Jesus, we soon discerned, would focus our minds and energies on more demanding, boring, long-range things of which Christmas was only a reminder, a start. And the rewards were ambiguous at best and amorphous in any case.

It was Santa, not baby Jesus, that got piles of extra wood and chips on the porch the night before Christmas, that got every bucket and container filled with water brought from the springs, got the hogs slopped, the cows milked and the mules fed without our being told, that got the front and back yards swept clean without a fuss as to whose turn it was.

But now Santa is long gone, along with those exuberant and innocent childhood Christmases. So is the setting and that community of earthy people on the banks of Kings Creek. What's left of that

44

time and place are the memories and values—
though badly frayed at the edges—and the hard
challenge of a baby Jesus grown up.

COMPETING WITH JESUS
By Phil Racine

I do not know if I was the only child born on Christmas day in Brunswick, Maine, in 1941, but I would not be surprised if I was. Some of the nurses wanted my mother to name me Christmas, but my parents, sensible people with an eye to the future, settled on Noel not knowing that an ancestor in seventeenth century Quebec had borne that name. Franco Americans did not speak of ancestors beyond two generations; they had other things to worship. Especially fortunate for my family; after all, we were the Normans who stayed at home in 1066. We were farmers, not warriors, it seems.

Having spent many Christmas days in Maine—the snow against the deep green backdrop of towering evergreens and brisk cold made the North Pole almost familiar—the season had always been special and would have been even had I not been born on that day. But since I had been, I knew it was for me that Dad was unpacking all those lights, setting up the crèche scene with its handsome ceramic figures purchased in his youth and the wooden stable built by him, the fake snow, the bird of peace, the real straw, the small pieces of firewood, the ceramic animals, and the baby Jesus. Seeing all of it bathed in the glow of my father's light bulb painted red (among my earliest memories), I was not sure what it all meant, but I knew that it had to do with me. After all, I was conscious of the congratulatory smiles—they tousled my hair!—the presents heaped at my feet, the lights, colors, and sounds aimed at my enjoyment. Didn't everyone make a fuss? Didn't Mom bake a lot, my aunts and grandfather give me stuff, everyone sing looking directly at me all the time? Of course, it was, as they all told me, my birthday. That day belonged to me.

As the years passed, that day changed. My birthday became "Christmas Day," someone else's day. It did not, after all, belong to me but to "Jesus." A Roman Catholic elementary school education had taught me a lot about Jesus; one thing for sure, he was more important than I was. If there was anyone tougher with whom to compete, I did not know whom it might be. Even my middle name, Noel, ceased to help me lay claim to the day. As I aged and became aware of Christmas, the name Noel became lost in the clutter of "the season," devoid of its special character, now just odd, a kind of clever ploy on my mother's part as if she had purposely marked me in some vain effort to single me out.

I was disappointed that December 25 was actually mine only by default, only when everyone else had finished. The joy of presents received and gifts given being over—Oh, and by the way, happy birthday. Actually, my parents had always gone to great lengths to make the day special—my aunt baked a graham cracker crust lemon pie for my birthday—always a masterpiece. But there was no way anyone could fool me, I was horning in on someone else's day; all that church stuff, the special Mass, the huge crêche scene, the extra fancy robes on the priests and acolytes—all that was not for me but for Him. It was really His day, and I was lucky He had let me be born at all, never mind on His day.

49

Yet, despite the disappointment of the loss, the season has continued to have a special quality for me. As a youngster, I walked at night in the sharp, dry cold that grabbed at my mouth and throat with every breath, heard the crunch of snow and crack of rutted ice under my heavy boots, glanced from Christmas tree lights in darkened rooms to bulbed candles in every window, to outdoor lights in yard trees, on wreaths and outlining an occasional roof—everything, everywhere reflected on snow. That walk marked the season for me and continues fixed in my memory as part of a generalized feeling of well-being, sort of warm and fuzzy, like a well-groomed cat but without the attitude.

Perhaps it has turned out that way because in Spartanburg I reached my maturity and realized the competition didn't seem as important as it once had. All people share their birthdays with others; maybe not in such a prominent and overwhelming way, but they share them nevertheless. Maybe the decisive moment in the changing of my attitude occurred, and reoccurs whenever I see it again, when the Spartanburg *Herald-Journal* ran a photograph of my son, Russell, as he was depositing his letter to Santa Claus into "Santa's talking mail box." I took a lot of ribbing for that: letting my cute son be exploited by the crass, materialistic, Christmas-shopping-fever mongers. But I had a secret agenda, perhaps only realized in the remembering of it; Russell was mailing my pitiful self-concern to the North Pole and thus transforming Christmas into his and his sister's day. Without my even realizing it, I had made an imaginary pact with Jesus—He could have His day; I let it go. My little piece of the day, remembered by others and celebrated late in the afternoon, would be just fine. The day belonged to others, others who had come to me here, in this place. So unlike Christmas as it had been, these in Spartanburg (bleak and without snow— brown was not a color which, in my youth, I had associated with Christmas) were better than memory; they were home now, made so by what counted—my own family in my own place.

Christmas in Spartanburg
1863

51

"Around the library fireplace a perfect mob had gathered, for there hung the white stockings lumpy and bumpy with apples, oranges, candy, and nuts. We expected but little from Santa Claus, knowing how scant and meager his war time stock of goodies was. But he remembered us and we were happy."

*—From the journal of Mary Dodd Elliott, courtesy of the
Spartanburg County Regional Museum.*

MOTHER'S MASTERPIECE
By Anne Alexander Bain

"I wanted to paint her a masterpiece," I tell the stranger. His arm hangs over the rest, touching mine. He leafs through the pen and ink stationery. The empty mini-bottle slides down the tray table.

53

The flight attendant clears away all evidence of my insobriety. She pushes the arm rest button. I catapult into rigid uprightness. The lights of Spartanburg appear like grounded stars.

He tells me over whining hydraulics that he'd be happy as a hound on a hunt to get such a gift. He hopes she is, too. He hands me back my artwork.

I think of the scratchy writing in Mother's last letter.

Greenville-Spartanburg jetport pans by our window like a movie segment. The engines rev in reverse thrust and slow as we taxi. In yesteryears I walked the tarmac to waving family. They still wave, but from inside the terminal. I see them at ramp's end.

Sisters and nieces hug me, saying, "Merry Christmas!"

"Welcome home!" My father surprises me. I thought he'd be home with Mother. And there she is! Her smile lacks animation, but she is ambulatory.

I take a deep breath. My hug envelops her thinness.

Spartanburg is growing. Front-end loaders move Carolina clay along black highway. The Buick weaves through concrete barricades. "That's the BMW plant," Daddy points to the construction along I-85.

54

The flag at Milliken waves larger than I recall.

I note new Christmas billboards.

"Panthers" training home, says Daddy passing Wofford. Spartanburg's Flagstar looms large against the skyline. At Converse College, trees grown huge since childhood glow. The kids buy ice cream at Main Street Cafe and we navigate home through Christmas traffic.

Daddy's tree shines in the yard. As kids we helped him string the lights. Now he needs a ladder. Momma's wreath is missing from the front door. Daddy guides her up the steps. The arrangement on the entry table is orange, from Thanksgiving. The living room mantle is missing its crêche and stockings. My parents sit on the couch. The coffee table bears a dated "Southern Living," but no "Grinch," or "Scrooge."

Daddy's house tree is radiant, alive with decorations. It smells like damp forest. Our banter is soft in its glow. My cross-legged nieces busy themselves beneath branches, noting which boxes bear their names. Daddy plays carols. New speakers reverberate "Joy to the World." The melody tickles my growing-up memories.

"We need a David Ball or Marshall Chapman or Marshall Tucker Christmas CD," I say.

Mother retires, quiet as a specter, to her room. Her vitality is noticeably absent from our living room repartee. Daddy builds a fire. He stuffs more newspaper beneath the logs and blows the blaze with bellows. My sister says he's thwarting Santa.

I serve Beacon hash and tea from the kitchen. Mother's winter wine isn't simmering on the stove. But foods from friends labeled, "Merry Christmas" or "Thinking of You" or "Get Well Soon" are on every counter top and table. My sister makes cocoa for the kids.

Eventually Daddy mixes Brandy Alexanders. He says, "You haven't missed a Christmas yet," and I chink my frosty goblet with his. My sisters raise their glasses.

"To having everybody home," says Daddy. "Merry Christmas!"

Mother's annual nightgown isn't packaged on my bed. The quilt and sheets feel cold. Ajax, the cocker, is restless. I transgress and he curls into my arms. Sleep lurks but doesn't come.

Come morning, I search for Momma's Christmas mugs. Unsuccessful, I sip from an orange cup. She's up before sunrise, always, before anyone, before Ajax. But this morning—Christmas Eve—Mother sleeps late.

The doorbell begins to ring. "Merry Christmas!" I hear a voice, and then another tell a sister, a niece, or my father. Another package, then another appears beneath the tree. Mother is still sleeping.

Come dusk, a lifelong friend of Mother's lets herself in, and takes Christmas pudding to Mother's room. I hear them talking. At least, I hear the friend talking. Mom's friend is less merry as I wave goodbye from the front door. From the car window she says she hopes to see at least some of us at her party, before midnight church.

Carols from WSPA are the only sounds in the house. I grab a bowl and a spoon and head for Mother's room. She is propped on pillows in her robe.

"I've come for pudding," I say. The winter's light is fading through the skeletal trees outside her window. I climb onto the bed beside her. We smile like children and spoon the steamy pudding. I feel a sudden, overwhelming sense of gratitude.

On Christmas morning I pass around the bacon, coffeecake, and more hot pudding. Mother sits still in the rocking chair. I hand her my gift. The kids open ten presents in the time Mother unwraps my one. She holds the stationery up in the light.

"I wanted to paint you something good, like a masterpiece," I tell her, "but this is all I had time for." I nod at the pen and ink stationery.

"You're my masterpiece," she says. The words emerge thickly as though her tongue was anesthetized. A hush surrounds even the children. These are her only comprehensible words since I've been home.

"My family is my masterpiece," she speaks again.

57

Ajax nuzzles his face into her hand. He wags.

Mother's sudden and sentimental oratory is utterly unlike her, and I feel as if I've conjured her verbiage like some ghostly Dickensian undigested pudding.

Perhaps I, not Mother, not cancer's reprieve, fashion her utterance from a longing. Perhaps I miss the noisy joys of her cooking and singing and wrapping and readying for every proceeding Christmas. Perhaps I want to hear some crowning remark that will make this Christmas comprehensible.

"Joy to the World" resounds through our home. Daddy offers Mom more pudding and sits back down. I gaze ahead to my sisters, their husbands and kids, my father and mother, and I embrace what I sense is our last Christmas, all together. I think of those yet to come. Let heaven and nature sing.

59

Christmas in Spartanburg During the Civil War

"At Christmas Times during the Civil War, people in Union did not have luxuries at all . . . Charleston was blockaded, and even Spartanburg, which was not much larger than Union at that time, did not carry luxuries in her stores, either in food or wearing apparel."

—*From "American Life Histories: Manuscripts from the Federal Writers' Project 1936-1940."*

SILVER BELLS
By Suellen E. Dean

I found myself standing between racks of silk panties listening to the First Presbyterian hand bell choir. A dozen white-gloved women thrust their arms forward at just the right moments to produce a smooth, clear sound. No words. Just the crystal echo of bells.

61

I felt out of place, not because I was standing in the lingerie department of Carolina Cash listening to Christmas music but because I wasn't dressed properly. They were wearing bonnets, bustles, and white blouses buttoned to their chins. Outside the store, people were dressed for "A Dickens of a Christmas," and they strolled the sidewalks of downtown Spartanburg as if there were plenty of shops to shop.

Most nights, the small city is silent except for an occasional car motor and a distant siren. The old have memories of Aug. W. Smith's department store and fancy windows filled with Christmas decorations. But that was long ago. And people and places have since abandoned downtown and migrated west to the mall. Why were so many people here? Other than a few antique shops, finance companies, and furniture stores, downtown was dead, rising only to remembrances. But on this night something magical was happening. People around me were singing carols and perhaps imagining another downtown, "A Christmas Carol." A man in a tall dark suit and a tall hat gave me his last roasted chestnut from an open fire he was tending on the street corner. I clenched it tightly and went home. That was three years ago, and I still have the souvenir. I keep it in my desk drawer at work, and I take it out each December as reminder that I need to go downtown again.

62

It is strange that I should find my Christmas spirit in a downtown when I never had one growing up in a southern Alabama farming community. There were no sidewalks. We didn't go Christmas shopping, or caroling from house to house. We had only a post office, a general store, one blinking light, and a mayor who doubled as the chief of police. There were miles of fields between houses, and I did not know that there were other children my age until I started school at Wilmer Elementary. I didn't hear much about big cities until Mrs. Opal Peters' sixth-grade class. She introduced me to culture. I thought she knew everything because she could play the piano. Her favorite songs were about parades and sidewalks. She would line us up, from the shortest to the tallest so she could see us all, then march us to the cafeteria to practice for our annual holiday performance. In spring, she made us sing, "In your Easter bonnet, with all the frills upon it . . . You'll be the grandest lady in the Easter parade." Mrs. Peters made us practice until we knew every phrase. Her tall black beehive would wobble from side to side and her short, round body would balance precariously on her pointy shoes, while she checked to make sure that everyone's lips were moving, hers, fire-red, pressing out the words.

Mrs. Peters loved Christmas as much as she loved Easter. We dressed in reds and greens and sang a lively rendition of "Silver Bells." She sang it with such feeling that I could close my eyes and imagine another place, filled with lights, far from rows of corn and watermelon. Far from Wilmer.

It wasn't until I stumbled into a small town newspaper job that I discovered you don't have to go to a big city to find sidewalks and parades. I worked in small towns for a long time because I needed to be able to bump into a familiar face sometimes. It was important to me.

My first parade was in a small Alabama town near the Gulf Coast. Everyone who lived there turned out for the annual Christmas parade. I had to write about it. I was proud of my first parade article. I even took the photograph. I gave a detailed description of all eight floats and mentioned

63

how Mrs. Goodman, while playing Mary, fell off the back of the truck carrying the First Baptist Church's nativity scene. She survived the fall but with a bruised hip after limping about a mile back to the church parking lot. Apparently, no one noticed she was gone.

My second parade was in an even smaller town, Monroeville, Ala. The only reason I moved there was because of Harper Lee, who wrote "To Kill a Mockingbird." I naively hoped her talent would rub off on me; I would write one book and become famous. Instead, I learned how to write colorful accounts of weddings, the importance of getting the deceased's name right in the obituary column, and provided in-depth parade coverage.

64

By the time I got a job in Spartanburg, I was a seasoned parade reporter and could cover the event without actually attending it. I had witnessed more Shriners in overalls than the average small-town dweller might see in ten lifetimes. I had seen more politicians waving from the back seats of red Mustangs, more marching bands and more baton-twirlers than Mrs. Opal Peters could have ever sung about in all of her years teaching. I began to beg editors not to send me downtown.

"I'll do anything. I'll cover the police beat. But please don't throw me into another parade route. I'm tired of it," I insisted.

Then I had children and turned into senti-mental mush. I felt the need to share the excitement of parades and downtown with my three little ones. While other families start their season off with a trip to the mall to take snapshots of Santa as their children sit in his lap, I drag the family from the breakfast table the morning after Thanksgiving, and we find our same spot on the curb at Church and Main streets in downtown Spartanburg. Every year it's the same story. I buy three cones of cotton candy, and we huddle together trying to stay warm. I always complain about forgetting the blanket. By the time we spot the red dot in the distance, my children have crawled under my clothes and are rubbing their sticky, little hands against my skin, trying to generate some heat. They usually want to go home. "After we see Santa," I promise.

"Why is Santa riding in a fire truck?" one of my little ones usually asks.

When we've all waved at him, we head over to Silver's discount to take advantage of the Christmas goodies. Everyone gets a dollar, and we spend an hour or so digging through the decorations and poring over the candy, the chocolate-covered cherries, the strands of candy canes, and the rows of red mesh stockings. Then we go home and make cups of hot chocolate, and the children talk me into putting up a Christmas tree.

Another annual tradition, at least for the last three years, has been our trip downtown to the "Dickens" celebration. I'm usually the first to find the hand bell choir. Storefronts that are lifeless in

65

the daytime come alive on this night as young ballerinas twirl around in them all night long. Carolers stroll along the streets. For one night, Spartanburg resembles an English village. One year we took the carriage ride. The sound of the mules' clicking hooves carried the beat as I hummed Mrs. Peters' song, "People laughing. People passing. Greeting smile after smile." After the ride, we had enough money left to buy a peach cobbler and hot chocolates topped with mounds of whipped cream. We stood under Spartanburg's tallest building and waited for the grand finale, the lighting of the 35-foot Frasier fir. I blew on my chocolate and watched the steam disappear into the night air, as the children danced around me in circles in the shadows. People kept coming to the plaza until we were all touching shoulders with strangers. I was pushed to the base of the tree and branches rubbed against my face. With the flick of a switch and the resulting blast of color reaching into the air, the crowd sighed. Everyone's eyes were on the tree as if we were there trying to count all the lights, an impossible task.

66

The crowd stood frozen in the lights for an endless second. And I felt a tiny tug on my sleeve. My eyes refocused on the ground. It was my nine-year-old daughter, Chelsea.

"Okay, you've seen the lights. Can we please go home? I'm tired of this," she pleaded, a ring of chocolate around her lips. We walked along the sidewalk to our car, pushing past the people, "Silver Bells" echoing in my ears.

67

KEEPSAKE
By Ruth Shanor

She was dainty, vivacious, and witty. Speaking softly in her natural Southern drawl, she made a place for herself for fifty years in Yankee-land. With subtlety and charm she manipulated friends and family to keep the attention on herself. She was my mother, born in Spartanburg, South Carolina, in 1901. She was everything I am not. I both loved her and hated her for those differences. Though Mom died many years ago, I find her in my thoughts more than ever this Christmas.

69

Mom was hard to compete with because Dad worshipped her blindly. I stayed out of her playing field during my adult life. Now that she is gone and I am alone, I find myself celebrating Christmas in Mom's home territory. I never thought that I would establish a home and buy a burial plot in upstate South Carolina. Yet, that is what my parents did after Dad retired many years ago. He brought her home.

Of course Christmas is family time. I'm acknowledging that my family roots are stronger than I ever imagined. Yes, Christmas is family time; though the family barely exists except in memories and stories, in bits of paper and broken chairs . . . perhaps a gaudy Christmas card sent as an afterthought.

We never came to Grandma Gentry's house for Christmas when I was a kid. It was too far, the roads were bad, and Dad had to work. Spartanburg was special for our summer visits, however, when watermelons were ripe and chickens were frying size. The automobile trip took at least two days from New York or Cincinnati or Pittsburgh—wherever we were living that year. We'd stop at a farm house along the way to spend the night. I would beg Dad not to stop at a farm if they didn't have a pony.

Grandma Gentry always sent a wonderful Christmas box to us up north. There were homemade cookies wrapped in newspaper. There was divinity candy in a tin box made from Baker's cocoa. Sometimes she sent molasses taffy. One year she made me a little apron just like Mom's. The surprise was finding a penny sewed in one pocket and a stick of chewing gum in the other.

After 1936 I never returned to Spartanburg until Mom and Dad retired here in 1958. Meanwhile my own little family celebrated Christmases in California, Utah, Pennsylvania, Kansas, Oklahoma, Texas, and Illinois. The houses kept changing, though the ornaments were the same each year. Finally even the people were farther and farther away from each other and then the ornaments were gone. This year my children and their children celebrated Christmas on three different continents. I wonder where they will find their roots.

When I sold my parents' home in Spartanburg, I saved enough of their furniture to make my mobile home in Cowpens livable. Dear Old Dad's five-foot walnut desk dominates my bedroom. Mom's curved channel back chair presides over the living room. This winter, however, the springs ripped through the bottom of the chair. The delicate gold tapestry had turned orange with Carolina dust. Dog hair was wedged into the tufted back. The sight of Mom's chair, ragged and lopsided, embarrassed me. Mom was a fastidious person.

I couldn't decide whether to replace it with a sturdy captain's chair or have it reupholstered. After all, who would I be saving it for?

As the Christmas season approached I thought more and more about my own heritage—that mixture of genes and education and life experiences that shaped me. I saw clearly that each of us makes his own connections. I cannot and should not limit my children's concept of how they arrived where they are. That is their riddle to solve. What is beautiful and comfortable to me may not be valu-

71

able to someone else. What represents my mother to me has become my treasure.

I hadn't realized how powerfully Mom influenced me. Whether I was rebelling against her or adoring her, I needed Mom exactly the way she was. I need her still. The jealousy disappeared a long time ago while the appreciation and compassion grew.

A week before Christmas I made my decision. Mom rode my shoulder to the upholstery shop to help me pick her kind of fabric. It is dainty and vibrant, the way she was. As a tribute to myself and to her I made Mom's chair new again.

72

Now in the late winter afternoons, I love coming into my little home where I flop down on the living room carpet. Duke and Dutchie, my two canine companions, turn themselves around in a few circles before curling up at the doorway. They know that this is quiet time. In silence we make brief eye contact and then I nod to the presence of Mom in her lovely chair. Peace and acceptance settle over my little family in Cowpens. We are home.

73

Christmas in Spartanburg
1863

"The Holidays were fast drawing to a close. In a short time the
soldier boys would be returning to duty. They were in fine health
and spirit. They seemed to have forgotten their wounds.
Though John Carson still limped.

—*From the journal of Mary Dodd Elliott, courtesy of the*
Spartanburg County Regional Museum.

MISTLETOE

By John Lane

"Mama, the old Druid's back again." I try the joke every year when I see the old man in the aging Chevy van pull up to my mother's house on Briarcliff Road. I know from Christmas past he's here to gather mother's mistletoe from the water oak in the front yard. I watch as the old man and his grandson get out of the van, remove a long yellow pole from the ladder rack, and begin poking at the oak's branches. They've done it so many years they don't even have to ask.

I'm an English professor and I can't help but see a Druid priest with his golden sickle working down the holy wondrous mistletoe for solstice two weeks away. Though I was raised a Methodist, I see the silver branch of the Celtic poets in the tiny white lights, the birthing goddess in the egg nog, and smell yule in the pungent Christmas tree.

For the ancient Druids mistletoe was the life-essence, a divine substance, all healing, immortality. As neither tree nor shrub, the evergreen mistletoe symbolizes that which is neither one nor the other, which by extension is the realm of freedom from limitations. Hence comes our custom of standing under mistletoe. In that space we, like the mistletoe, are free from restrictions of convention.

I love thinking about how the pagan world, the old nature worship, flows like a powerful river just below all our modern religions and mythologies. As Simon Schama says in *Landscape and Memory*, "The cults which we are told to seek in other nature cultures . . . are in fact alive and well and about us if only we know where to look for them." But I'm at my mother's to put up the decorations, not speculate to myself about pagan nature rituals.

My sister Sandy is looking for the decorations upstairs, my brother-in-law is asleep in the recliner despite all the noise, my niece is in the kitchen with Mother warming the food for lunch, my nephew watches a basketball game, and his wife tries to calm their two girls, hyper with the smell of Christmas in the air.

Somebody puts on a stack of old 45s and we really know Christmas is on the way: Alvin & the Chipmunks singing "Christmas Time is Here," "The Little Drummer Boy," BA-RA-PA-BUM-BUM, and of course, "Snoopy's Christmas." When the last record drops, the Red Baron says, "Merry Christmas, my friend," as Snoopy flies away to the sound of Christmas bells.

I've only missed one Christmas at home in over forty years, so I know, after Snoopy sings, it's time to decorate; Sean's girls unwrap the plastic baby Jesus, sheep, camels, and toothpick manger that I unwrapped when I was a boy, thirty years ago; Sandy asks as always where the tree will go. As always, we tell her in the corner. I'm finally distracted from the window for good when I remember how much I love the little sweet pickles Mama puts on the Christmas tray.

These family rituals of decoration are ancient mysteries too. Maybe family is a little like mistletoe, a juncture between who we are and who we can be. I know for sure that at its best family offers a deep freedom. I can feel it as I watch another Christmas taking shape in front of my eyes.

My mother finally comes in from the kitchen, and looks out the window as the old man picks up the last of the mistletoe.

"Oh him? He's no Druid," she laughs, standing next to me at the window. "He's a mill worker who sells that mistletoe every year to rich people up near Banner Elk."

With the business finished in the yard, the boy brings mistletoe to the front door and knocks. "Granddaddy says there's good berries this year. If you want it, there's more." Mama smiles. "It's always our first Christmas gift," she says, and hangs a fresh green sprig about our front door.

EPIPHANY AND THE TREE
By Barbara Cobb

When I was young, I associated the Christmas tree with Santa and bows and lots and lots of gifts. But it also served as a link to the lowly manger, and particularly with the long-awaited arrival of the Wise Men, who bring gifts for God's son. The connection is somewhat loose, but it made sense to me: my mother always topped the tree with a great big gold filigreed star, and Dad rigged it so that the very last bulb on the light string shone from behind it; my incipient metaphorical mind read this as a sign. To me, the tree symbolized the vigil and the voyage that leads to baby Jesus, much as the stockings hung by the chimney with care symbolized another vigil and voyage—of a large red-suited, jelly-bellied man and a sack full of everything I had circled in the Sears Wish Book.

The first Christmas after I moved to

79

Spartanburg, it took a bit to get into the Christmas spirit, mostly because I wasn't accustomed to what seemed to me an unseasonable holiday season of near-seventy degree daytime temperatures and sweaty Santas with kids in holiday T-shirts on their laps. Eventually, the weather cooled a bit and the brown-wrapped boxes of gifts from family Up North and Out West began to arrive. I decided I'd better do something. I wasn't feeling very spirited, but I had noticed that ours was the only house on the entire east side not belighted, beribboned, and begarlanded. I was still feeling barren of Christmas spirit, but there was no reason to drag down the whole neighborhood, waiting for me to start feeling ho-ho, not ho-hum.

80

I'd seen a lovely tree lot on Pine Street, by the Y. But when I got there, there was no corral of happy trees and happy bemittened children chasing around their sap-oozing trunks; there was nothing, not an oil-drum-fire-bin, not a two-by-four, not a length of string, not a pine needle. So I scoured Spartanburg for a hold-out tree-seller, and worked my way through Lyman and Greer and Taylors; finally, somebody at a filling station told me that somebody's brother-in-law was still working a lot in Greenville. Sure enough, just beyond the mall, fifteen lonely trees trying to look casual lounged around the perimeter of an immense corral. A huge happy man with a bushy red beard, very red cheeks, a rather besmirched Santa hat, and a green hunting jacket, accepted my ten-dollar bill with thanks and praise for my generosity, and helped me load one into my station wagon.

I took home a tree with a lot of character. That night, I hung brand-new lights and Wal-Mart-purchased balls on the stork-like, slightly-browning evergreen. I hadn't been able to find a star for its top; the broken-winged angel that I'd found in the discount room at the back of the mall Christmas shop would have to do. She was pink and blue and white when I brought her home. My husband said no. After I nail-polished her red and green and gold, he relented. I had John string the last light just as Dad used to, lighting the wayward angel, but I didn't think she or the tree looked much like a beacon for kings. I felt like the joy part of Christmas was falling right along with the puny tree's needles.

My mother-in-law dropped by while I was arranging the all-one-size Wal-Mart balls. She handed me a giant dog-eared cardboard box, and told me that she'd downsized to a piano-top tree years ago and thought her ornaments might find a good home here. She didn't even flinch when she saw the Charlie Brown tree in the corner. I was gladdened by her thoughtfulness and her toleration, and I felt quite a bit better. As she and John chatted, I opened the box, and the many little boxes it contained. In each box, I found wonderful, colorful ornaments, beautiful ornaments that I felt I'd

81

known all my life, ornaments that made me feel at
home, here in my new home. I felt that smooth
marble of sentiment in my throat, and the dull cloud
of teariness rise from my heart to my head.

Not only were they beautiful, but also they
were exactly like the ornaments that my mother
and father have hung each year at my childhood
home. Here were the bells and the birds and the
old glass drums, the red-and-gold teardrops, the
glitter-adorned balls, the cornucopiae. Even the
bird-cage-shaped plastic things with the little tin
windmills inside. I fought the tears and concen-
trated on placing those plastic things carefully, each
above a light so the vague heat from those cool bulbs
might make its windmill spin. Whether they do or
not is one of those issues one doesn't raise, much
like how Santa enters a home without a chimney.
To me, they spun, and the exhilaration of childhood Christmas became alive again, to accompany
and complete the grown-up solemn joy of this holy
season. The angel felt it too: suddenly she looked
like a herald, and Jesus was almost here.

We took the tree down on the Tuesday after
Epiphany, once I was sure that the angel had greeted
all three of the Kings. I packed each of those beautiful ornaments, along with their angel friend, into
a newer cardboard box, labeled it "Christmas," and
carried it to the attic, where it waits to fill me with
Christmas joy—and my family's love—as we greet
the baby Jesus year after year.

82

Christmas near Pauline
1864

83

"December 25: It is not a merry Christmas to me.
True, I am in a comfortable house with the comforts of life
plentiful around me, and the family are all well and happy,
but the 'Head of the family, the King of the household' is now
in the Confederate camp exposed to the Yankee shells."

—Journal entry by Eliza Liles Harris from "Piedmont
Farmer:- The Journals of David Golightly Harris
1855-1879," edited by Philip N. Racine.

12

THE CHRISTMAS STICK
By Betsy Wakefield Teter

85

The Christmas Stick stands six feet tall. Plucked from the narrow cane patch beside the house, it slouches toward the driveway, its branches no more than twigs. My two young sons have planted it here, like a scarecrow among the ornamentals, securing it with a stack of broken bricks. This year, in addition to a string of twenty-two lights looped around its stunted limbs, the Christmas Stick wears a yellow construction paper star whose five points folded up into a fist after the first rain. Its electric cord snakes through the mulch, crosses the front porch and plugs obtrusively into an outlet next to the door.

For the past three years, trimming this "tree" has been the way Rob and Russell have christened the holiday season. It is their idea, their tree, with their decorations. It is their own little shrine to the notion that Christmas is really for kids.

A shrine with, heaven forbid, *colored* lights.

Here in my Spartanburg neighborhood of historic homes, well-kept bungalows and old-money mansions, there is an unspoken holiday aesthetic code: Christmas lights are white—preferably tiny and white. They grace the dogwoods and the grand entranceways with a homogeneity that is beautiful, simple, and seductive. The miniature white lights carry a seamless theme of good taste and old tradition from house to house, from block to block, from street to street.

There is nothing tasteful about the Christmas Stick. By day, it looks like a dead branch yanked to earth by a tangled green rope. By night, it appears as if a rogue strand of lights from some other neighborhood has been carried by the wind and deposited, unceremoniously, on an unsuspecting bush. Whatever the time of day, it causes double takes from people passing by in their cars.

I don't remember how or why it went up the first year. We own no white lights at our house, my quiet rebellion against the conformity around us. I've never been much of a joiner. So when the children chose to illuminate their creation, they used a colored strand borrowed from the indoor tree. I fought that sudden feeling of conspicuousness and told myself the kids deserved their fun. The Teters would celebrate Christmas in Technicolor.

But on those nights when they forgot to plug

it in, no one said anything. Their tree stayed dark and inoffensive.

There wouldn't have been a Christmas Stick at all last year if we adults had had our way. As December rolled around and the boxes of ornaments and figurines were lugged from the basement, their father whispered to me, "Let's make sure the kids don't do that bamboo tree in the front yard again."

"Good idea," I whispered back and cringed. "Geez, that was awful."

Two afternoons later, the kids and I were shuffling through a stack of old photographs, looking for a specific shot to accompany a school project. Up came the picture of the boys in their Power Ranger superhero outfits and their plastic talking swords, posing like militant elves in front of the previous year's Christmas Stick.

Oh no, I thought.

"Mom, we have to do that again!" Russell shouted, leaping from his seat and disappearing around the corner. When I caught up with him, his six-year-old arms were full of Christmas-light spaghetti. Colored bulbs burst against the hardwood floor as he hopped up and down, babbling about his tree.

I tried to stall by making the process seem too difficult and lengthy to accomplish in the short period of time before basketball practice was to start. My idea was to put it off until tomorrow and

87

maybe they would forget all about it.

"Look," I started, "we'd have to find the right piece of bamboo and then we'd have to cut it down. Bamboo is hard to cut down. We'd need some kind of saw, and I have no idea where one is. The garage is a mess.

"There just isn't time," I tried.

Before I could finish my case, they had dashed out the front door. There, at the corner of the house, was the perfect Christmas Stick, already disconnected from its tricky bamboo root system. Not green enough so that the leaves were still on it, but not so dry that the limbs broke off when the lights were added. They jabbed it like a flag of victory into the very spot where its predecessor stood the year before.

The resurrection had begun.

I sat quietly on the front steps and watched the Christmas Stick take shape. Oblivious to everything around them, the boys worked in tandem, tackling this job with all the seriousness of surgeons. They wrapped and reached and clipped. The longer I watched them work, the more clearly I recognized their tree for what it really is. It is uncensored Christmas joy. This quirky little Christmas tradition was all theirs, emerging like a sapling through the still-warm winter earth. I felt no tug to drive to Wal-Mart and buy white lights. I felt no need to steer them with their colored lights to one of the real trees in the yard. No grinch was going to steal

88

the Christmas Stick. Especially not a grinch named Mom.

Tonight, as I look out the front window of my house, I see Converse Heights through the glow of multi-colored lights. The Christmas Stick is back in full glory for a third run, and I like the statement it makes. I've come to treasure this wacky little affront to community Christmas standards.

Still, I have no idea whether the Christmas Stick truly has taken root at my house. Perhaps next year Rob and Russell will forget all about it. Perhaps they'll think it was foolish or be worried about being late for basketball practice. Childhood pastimes, after all, tend to disappear with the speed of a South Carolina snow.

89

But for this year, the Christmas Stick will be lit every night as darkness falls.

Even if I'm the one who has to do it.

GLORIA IN EXCELSIS DEO!

By Ann Hicks

I am standing at the window looking out, morosely observing the absence of snow. The calendar says that it is December 5th, 1957, and in Hungary—where I came from eleven months ago—snow will have blanketed Budapest by now.

I am thinking that the following day, the 6th of December, Santa Claus, or as we call him, Mikulas, arrives there. Just about this time, Hungarian children are polishing their shoes or getting their bedroom slippers ready and placing them on the windowsill. Mikulas arrives sometime during the dead of night, along with his useful devil, Krampus, and leaves wonderful chocolates and candy in the footwear. Sometimes though, he leaves a little bunch of twigs instead of the sweets—they are pretty twigs, either silver or gold-colored. They are stuck into the shoes of those who are misbehaving at the time. Krampus keeps up with that list.

This custom offers a wonderful opportunity for parents as a device of discipline: "You better straighten out, or Mikulas will tell the baby Jesus not to send you any presents!" This works very nicely, and for at least eighteen days before Christmas most parents experience a blessed peace of mind. I think of my own childhood and how I could be counted upon to be good, at least during those days of anticipation. Somehow I *knew* that these two gift-givers worked for the same company. They talked to each other about bad kids; they knew all about kids like me.

I snap back to reality. Now a mother of two babies, one twenty months old and the other three months old, I wonder what our first Mikulas and Christmas will be like in this new world of Spartanburg, South Carolina. I turn from the window, picking up the day's newspaper and turning its pages absent-mindedly. Somewhere in there two words catch my eyes: "Christmas Parade." I am transfixed. This is most intriguing! Although my knowledge of the English language is minimal, I know exactly what the words mean. Only, I have no idea as to whom will be parading for Christmas and why.

As I am accustomed to doing, I begin to painstakingly translate each and every word with the help of my Hungarian-English pocket dictionary which I had bought in the refugee center in

Camp Kilmer, New Jersey. The more I translate, the more confused I become as to the meaning and purpose of this occasion. Nothing makes sense; what does Santa Claus (a.k.a. Mikulas) have to do with Christmas? The saint is in the habit of coming to visit children on his nameday—St. Nicholas Eve—which falls on December 6th. The baby Jesus sends gifts on the eve of his birthday, December 24th. Surely everyone knows that! They are two distinct holidays.

The article goes on to state that this is going to be a huge parade with "48 marching units." I look up "units" and I look up "marching." The former has to do with measurements, the latter with military precision. How can these units march? There will also be lots of beauty queens, it states. I know those two words as well. I have seen them at home in western-style magazines. Still, what do they have to do with Christmas? The most astonishing part comes at the last of the article. There will be fourteen high school bands "serenading Mr. Kringle." What! Here is the Mikulas of my children *being serenaded*! For me, serenades mean an expression of romantic love. What mystery!

I have a dilemma. I do not like this mixing of two separate holidays. What does this mean for me and my little kids, Attila and Patricia? How will I teach them about the wonderful customs of their ancestors? I become very sad and tearful and lonely. I recall how previously my twenty-two-year-

93

old husband was quoted in this very newspaper as to why we came here: "To establish a new home, to begin a new life." Does that mean that I have to adopt the strange habits of the natives?

Our family had fled Hungary on November 28th, 1956, and arrived in the United States on the last day of January 1957. The 1956 Hungarian Revolution of October 23rd had drowned in blood, tearful curses, and recriminations, and scattered 200,000 of us to four corners of the world. We had become political refugees. At age eighteen I was a traveling member of a great Diaspora, along with my twenty-one-year-old husband and nine-month-old baby boy, Attila.

America's shores lap up her new wave of refugees, and deposit them into safe little tidal pools. Ours happens to be Spartanburg. It is where I will be spending my first Christmas in the New World. Oh America! How I dreamt of this land of glamour, movie stars, and skyscrapers—my expectations knew no bounds. Alas, reality is a whole lot more complex. This small Southern town has neither glamour nor skyscrapers. Additionally, I do not speak the language, and have no clues about the prevailing customs.

Later that afternoon I write a letter to my mother:

Sweet Mother,
I have to tell you that I'm very unhappy. I'm homesick, and it doesn't help that in this country it is not

the little Jesus who gives the gifts on Christmas Eve. It is Santa Claus. Imagine this: there is actually a parade today in his honor with beauty queens, and he is being serenaded.

Earlier this afternoon I turned on the television, and saw Santa advertising gifts from a local furniture store! What little I could understand of what was being said had to do with dollars. Sweet Mommie, I feel as though I've fallen into a deep crevice—"katyuba estem."

What should I do about the Christmas of my children? Tell me, do I give up the little Jesus for the old fat guy from the North Pole? I don't even want to think about this right now.

I go on to talk about what a healthy baby Patricia is. She has gained two pounds and ten ounces since her birth.

My mother's reply comes swiftly from Budapest. "My darling little one . . . " she says. Her soothing words lie on the paper like her fine and fancy embroidery on a pillow. She writes with middle-aged sensibilities about creating new traditions from the old ones and reserving judgment for a later day. "Gather happy thoughts," she says. "An armful of those will last you for a long time," then she adds pragmatically, "until after Christmas anyway."

Family photos of the Christmas of 1957 show a happy little family gathered around the tree on Christmas Eve. Brightly colored packages are being opened, and I'm seen beaming with joy in many of the pictures.

95

Memory is recreated into peace and exultation. Gloria in Excelsis Deo!

**Christmas near Pauline
1865**

97

"December 25: Christmas morning. Damp, clouddy
day, wet & drizly, but otherwise warm & pleasant ... The
negroes leave today to hunt themselves a new home while
we will be left to wait upon ourselves. It may be a
hardship, but I hardly think it will."

—*From "Piedmont Farmer: The Journals of David Golightly
Harris 1855-1879," edited by Philip N. Racine.*

SECOND COMING
By Linda Powers Bilanchone

ithin the sound of the bells of Spartanburg's downtown churches but out of sight of Main Street's propriety, St. Joseph Catholic Church awaits a second coming. To reach St. Joseph's, the Sunday churchgoer walks west on Duncan Street, passing an abandoned cemetery whose monuments stretch for blocks, their granite presence barely able to penetrate the tangled grasses which surround them. On the other side of the street, the sturdy square World War II houses of Camp Croft Courts march by stiffly, brick by brick. Then the sidewalk ends and the way opens to reveal a modest white church with a broad front porch, presiding over seven acres of mowed field and pine groves. Marking a rhythm which continues past the church are the flagpole and a white-washed statue of Joseph and the child Jesus set in the middle of the field.

99

At the far end of the field is the parsonage, a brick ranch house which signals the pedestrian's return to the urban world.

When my family and I moved to Spartanburg in 1972, "Spartanburg's Catholic Church" was pointed out to us: St. Paul the Apostle Catholic Church on Dean Street. No one mentioned St. Joseph's; probably no one knew about it. It had been established as a mission to the African-American community in 1940. Over the years, the black congregation had welcomed whites and by the early seventies, the congregation was half black and half white. When we discovered the church, its low-peaked roof and modest four walls sheltered parishioners who had consciously sought it out.

Because we were small, everyone participated in the life of the church. We prepared the altar; we learned music for the liturgy; we built cabinets and mowed the lawn. We lectured and ushered and sang. We served on the parish council and served meals. We created our own Stations of the Cross for Lent. One year they were fabric and newspaper; another year our resident artist, Buzz, painted a Resurrection scene and others carved crosses of wood. We gazed at our handiwork each Friday night as we said the stations, shuffling from one to another, spilling over into the previous station because the space between them was so small.

Our existence was a marvel. Perhaps that's why we kept inviting the world in. We indulged in music and art and literature and poetry. Our pastor, Peter Clarke, believed that humankind is becoming and that the arts are an essential and glorious part of that becoming. We studied Job using the poetry and engravings of William Blake and readings from Archibald MacLeish's play, "J.B." We sponsored a Thomas Aquinas seminar on the 700th anniversary of his death with a panel of visiting philosophy professors. Wofford College Theater Workshop students performed Samuel Beckett's "Endgame" right there in our midst. With wonder, we watched actors emote from ashbins. We asked ourselves, "What does this mean?" "Why are we doing this?" Then we tried to answer our own questions as we sat in a circle to talk about the play.

101

If the world didn't count us in as its routine unfolded, we counted ourselves in. When an exhibit by the South Carolina-born African-American artist William H. Johnson was shown at the Arts Center, Peter borrowed two paintings and brought them to St. Joseph's so that our parishioners could see them. They were placed in front of the altar so that everyone could come forward and inspect them carefully; learn from them; admire them; find pride or solace in them.

And Christmas was no different. We put up the small tree with blinking lights. We gathered magnolia leaves and pine boughs to place around the statues of saints, some light-skinned, some dark. We put candles in the windows. We practiced chant evoking St. Peter's in Rome and the African-American hymn, "Kum Ba Yah."

Midnight Mass was charged with energy. The dark starry sky seemed to close in on the tiny building; we seemed to be the only people in the world celebrating the birth of Christ. Why were we the chosen ones? We were Flora and Columbus and Bennie and Hattie. We were Frances and Susie. Jim. Norb. George. Ila.

One Christmas was special for its poetry, which spoke in plain language of the way things are. Barbara Ferguson, a fine actress and reader, recited Lawrence Ferlinghetti's poem, "Christ Climbed Down," while her son, Michael, used slide projectors to fill our small space with images of the birth of Christ punctuated by photographs of homeless people. When Barbara said, "Christ climbed down from His bare tree this year and ran away to where there were no rootless Christmas trees hung with candy canes and breakable stars," we paid attention. We hoped that there were no candy canes or breakable stars in sight. As Barbara invoked Ferlinghetti, we disavowed "powderblue Christmas trees hung with electric candles and encircled by tin electric trains and clever cornball relatives." As Barbara peered over her glasses and spoke with measured conviction, we suddenly wanted nothing to do with "Sears Roebuck crèches" or "televised Wise Men." Barbara was British, and every word she uttered possessed a power that rivaled melody.

When she read, we listened. We listened deeply. Her gift was our gift; we praised God for it. And so she and Ferlinghetti went on, on that beautiful Christmas day. And then the sweet moments of becoming came to an end as Barbara intoned:

Christ climbed down
from His bare Tree
this year
and softly stole away into
some anonymous Mary's womb again
where in the darkest night
of everybody's anonymous soul
He awaits again
an unimaginable
and impossibly
Immaculate Reconception
the very craziest
of Second Comings

103

Note: On Sunday, August 18th, 1996, the last Mass was said in that small space which was ours. After fifty-six years of witness, St. Joseph Catholic Church has stolen softly away to await a second coming.

Campobello Christmas
By Gloria Underwood

105

My parents grew up mostly in northern Spartanburg County, so our Christmases here go back several generations. Their entire married life had been spent in Campobello where they reared four children. As the oldest, I can remember the gradual twelve-year expansion: first a brother, then two sisters. With each Christmas, more and more gifts would appear under the tree until we finally outgrew the little house within the Campobello city limits.

When I was thirteen, we moved from "downtown" Campobello to some acreage left over from my father's old homeplace, about two miles out. That part of the county is becoming more desirable now, more inhabited, but in the mid 1960s, it was pretty remote.

Things are different out in the country. They were then; they are now. Everybody knows everybody else and most of their relatives; you always wave when you see somebody; it's quiet and very dark at night. My parents' home is surrounded by about twenty acres of land. There's no question of spying on the neighbors; we can't even see the roads leading to our property. The nearest residence is close enough for comfort, but far enough away for comfort, too. Because our house is on a hill, we have clear visibility of the surrounding area in the winter when the trees have shed their leaves, and with some imagination we can even see as far as the creek a quarter mile away. Far from feeling isolated, we reveled in the open spaces; instead of falling asleep to the roar of trucks on the Asheville Highway, we drifted off to the calls of crickets and whippoorwills.

From the year I moved into my first Spartanburg apartment after college graduation, I have continued to spend Christmas Eve at home. My first visit to the Christmas Eve midnight service at First Presbyterian Church in Spartanburg with my high school sweetheart began a personal tradition of attendance, initially, and participation, eventually, in that program. Since I was seventeen, I have traveled that road from Spartanburg to Campobello at 1:00 a.m. every Christmas morning but three, sometimes accompanied, more often not, in order to wake up "at home" on Christmas Day.

By 12:30 a.m., Spartanburg shuts down; every store, restaurant, filling station closes. The six or seven cars on the road thin out to none as I head toward the outer reaches of the county. (Most recently, one of the convenience stores was open all night, and I did see three or four cars; my sisters suggested that Santa must have needed a Bud Light and a Salem!) On clear nights, the sky seems lit by stars. Some years, I'm convinced I've seen a red twinkling light way up, moving slowly as if leading a tremendous effort. Music enhances my pilgrimages: the Hallelujah Chorus may be in order or Aaron Neville crooning "Silent Night." Earlier years, Bonnie Raitt or R.E.M. would have rocked me home.

An occasional siren in the distance reminds me of another Christmas Eve twenty-something years ago when my brother, Philip, was a student at Furman University, my sisters, Sylvia and Denise, were still at Chapman High School, and I was living on my own. All of us were at home except Dad, who was still at work; it was early afternoon and we each had some project: cleaning the house, baking cookies, last-minute wrapping—those holiday things. Mom had gone outside to gather evergreens, magnolia leaves, and nandina berries for her centerpiece.

The carols playing softly in the background were suddenly interrupted by Mom bursting through the door, slamming it behind her, yelling, "Lock the doors! Lock the doors! They's a convict loose." (If you live in northern Spartanburg County, then you recognize and employ that most useful grammatical construction, "They's . . . ." It's efficient, doubling as "there is . . . " and "there are . . . " and serving other usages that I haven't quite deciphered.) We came running, eager to learn what had propelled Mom so vociferously into our midst.

Breathless, she gasped, "It's the helicopter and the sirens. They musta found 'em."

Still puzzled at her words, we decided to find out for ourselves. But that meant going outside, and that meant opening the door.

"Don't touch that door. You can't go outside. And while you're here, pull the drapes."

"Mom," one of us begged, "calm down and tell us what you are talking about."

Looking at us as if we had taken leave of our senses, she finally explained. It seems that whenever there is an escape from one of the local correctional institutions, the loose convicts head for a creek. The bloodhounds can't trace them in the water, and the escapees can hunker down under the overhanging brush that conveniently hides them— never mind that this was winter. Either the county police or SLED would send helicopters flying surveillance over the creeks in the area to try to locate the freedom seekers.

Once we finally decoded what she was saying, we were merciless. We laughed; we scoffed; we rolled our eyes and shook our heads and went back to our tasks. Concern for her brood and her nest uppermost in her mind, Mom found herself an inside job and didn't go outside the rest of the afternoon. We did, however, catch her looking out the windows from time to time.

But the first announcement on the news that Christmas Eve stopped us in our tracks. There had been a break-out at one of the local institutions; three men had escaped and were heading north. Our imaginations ran rampant: Didn't those local hoodlums from junior high finally get caught for stealing cars? Hadn't they been put in the slammer? Two of them were brothers. They must have escaped to spend Christmas with their poor mother who lives right in Campobello! And they took their friend with them—in the spirit of the season, of course. Hadn't Mom heard sirens, too?

109

Reluctantly convinced, we accepted her smug countenance and her I-told-you-so demeanor as she said, self-righteously, "Maybe next time they's a helicopter and sirens, you'll believe me." And we celebrated Christmas with a notably paltry centerpiece that year.

A piece at a time, the real story was revealed. It came out later that a high school buddy of mine with a Santa Claus girth had dressed as St. Nick, and some of his fellow volunteer firemen had agreed to ride him around the Campobello community in the fire truck as a Merry Christmas wish from the fire department. As these tales go, somebody knew somebody with a helicopter who agreed to fly over the Santa truck, following them on their rounds, just in case the fire sirens weren't enough. The ruckus was simply a Campobello Merry Christmas; the convicts had been apprehended only a short distance from the scene of the breakout.

Having passed through the northern edges of Inman on these early morning treks, I watch the darkness intensify as I move farther into the country. Inexplicably, inevitably, I roll down the window to hear the quiet grow here in the dark. Neither whippoorwills nor crickets sing to me in these bleak midwinter hours; the tires hum steadily and sometimes the wind whispers.

A solitary figure, I hurry along, restful in the quiet night. I greet these Christmas mornings with gladness, feeling blessed to be from the foothills and graced by the glory, even in the dark, of nature. This, for me, is Christmas. And I know I'm home where the nights are darker, the world is quieter, and sometimes a siren just means Merry Christmas.

Christmas in Enoree
1896

III

"Our first Christmas at Enoree proved quite an experience
for me. The families of the president and the treasurer of the
mill celebrated in a lavish manner ... As we entered the large
drawing room there was a beautifully decorated cedar tree
almost covered with garlands of pop-corn, cranberries, and
imitation fruits. On the floor around the tree was a great
array of wrapped and unwrapped gifts. Everyone had
noisemakers and paper hats. The president's six children
had enough toys to open a small store."

—From "Out of Season" by Paul M. Allen, published by
VantagePress (1968).

LAST CHRISTMAS

By Butler E. Brewton

There is a house off Old Georgia Road southwest of Spartanburg where I lived as a boy in the county. That house is locked and deserted this December. The windows are covered, dusty, and bolted. The yard in which my father's special apple tree stood proudly for so many years is grown up with weeds and wild sprouts. Gray and faded barns lean, silently decaying. But I remember many seasons there, especially one particular Christmas. It was the Christmas after we'd buried my father in November 1978. We children had had to travel long distances to be back home with my mother that day, but we managed the journey, coming from Ohio, Maryland, Washington, and New Jersey. We sensed it would be our last Christmas together off Old Georgia Road.

"They'll be here soon," my mother said, wiping her hands on her apron as she looked up the road through the kitchen window. We sat circled around the breakfast table, each of us quietly tense about what was about to happen. It was Christmas Eve. The tree bought from the hardware store sparkled, and I could hear over the radio Mahalia Jackson moaning out the lyrics of "Little Drummer Boy." Her singing made me think about the Christmases when I was a child.

Back then our white-washed barns smelled of stored hams, sweet potatoes, and old harnesses put to rest since summer. We children would listen to ourselves sing carols my mother had taught us when we stood huddled together around her piano. And as the season aged ripe as holly berries, we tried to be our better selves so Santa Claus would not pass us by on Christmas morning. So we fed the hogs without having to be told, picked up wood chips near the chopping block, stayed outside in the cold doing all sorts of things until we were nearly frozen from head to toe.

Back then it seemed the sky was always gray on Christmas Eve, threatening snow or an ice storm. Mama and Daddy would head off to the town of Spartanburg. I did not know why, or maybe I did not dare to know why. Santa Claus could not afford too many questions about where your parents went on Christmas Eve. We children just took off for the woods behind the house and into the deep distance even beyond the barns and cow lot, always

114

muddy that time of year. My older brother led the way with an ax, a sister close behind with old rusty scissors and my father's dull hatchet. We went deep into the damp woods, sort of in a line, one behind the other. Cold and by ourselves, we searched for a special cedar and red-berry holly. When we spotted them, our young eyes gleamed with excitement. It was a thrill hacking the small tree down and snipping branches of holly loaded with red berries from the bush! The cedar needles and holly spines pierced our tender palms, but we didn't mind. We'd load our find on an old wooden sled, and in that cold gray woods we dragged both tree and holly home.

That night we'd light the seldom-lighted fireplace in the living room. It glowed red, sending heat out onto the hearth. We children decorated our tree with what we thought was pretty, using the old twisted garlands and half burnt-out string of bulbs we kept in a box from one year to the next. Then we stuck pieces of holly and cuts of cedar over the windows and doors, their odor mingling with the scent of my mother's sausage, freshly ground from hog killing a few days past. We slept through the night as best we could with our Santa boxes set in place in the dining room. It was a restless sleep beneath cold sheets, but our dreams were filled with tinsel and warm expectation.

We woke up early while it was still dark, hearing the cracking and popping of a fresh-lit fire.

115

Then creeping through dim rooms, we single-filed our way across the dark hall to see what Santa Claus had left in the dining room. Strange now, but my brother led us again, not with ax in hand but with a heavy stick designed to beat up Santa Claus should he still be hanging around in there. I never really did understand his plan to attack a fat man bearing gifts, but I remember so well the excitement of crossing that hall. The great anticipation was almost too much to bear. And then we saw it—that table on which our boxes had been set. Looming up in the dimness, were the gifts that Santa had left.

I remember, too, my box one certain Christmas. I'd wanted a bicycle I'd seen at Western Auto on Church Street, but inside my box was a cardboard replica of Noah's Ark and punch-out animals, two by two. But I joined the other children, taking turns showing our gifts off to each other and breaking them long before the morning light. My paper ducks finally wouldn't stand up anymore, but I held them in position with my hand.

"Quack, quack," I said for them. "Quack, quack." When other kids rode by on bright new bikes or drew their cap pistols from shiny holster belts to show me what their Santa had left them, I sat on the doorstep proudly holding up my own gift.

"Quack, quack," I spoke for my ducks. "Quack!"

But that was more than forty years ago. Now

we sat, still tender from loss, the experience with death, grownup children knowing we could never recapture an era gone. And when they came, those trucks and the bulldozer huffing and puffing into the driveway, we single-filed out into the yard. I helped my mother direct the bulldozer, and we all stood in a huddle, not around a piano to sing, but to watch the men work. The bulldozer pushed my father's personal barn over first, then that apple tree. I heard the roots breaking, snapping like old cords out of the ground. We watched that tree go over the hill, dead as a doornail, down towards the gully; and we knew we would never grow fruit trees again off Old Georgia Road. Neither would we go into the deep woods looking for real cedars and holly again. An era had passed, buried like the tree was when pushed into the gully and as painfully grievous as the burial of a father.

117

I followed the rest back into the house which had been remodeled many times. We talked about our careers and our special accomplishments back in the cities in which we now lived. But staring through the sliding doors, I wished again for the days of poverty that were so rich, wanting an ax, an old hatchet, rusty scissors, and just one more Noah's Ark. No one knew what had come over me, but I just couldn't help but to say aloud:

"Quack, Quack."

MAKING NEW MEMORIES
By Jane Mailloux

Every year since we've been in Spartanburg, we've packed up our family and left for Christmas in Canada. We would trek a thousand miles back to the Eastern Townships of Quebec to our small corner of Utopia . . . a little town nestled on the edge of the mountains with undulating hills and picture card winters. It always seemed on Christmas Eve we would leave the candlelight church service as big fat snowflakes came drifting down. And all of those sparkles that you see pasted on Christmas cards would be sprinkled right out at our feet.

119

It wasn't so much that we hurried away from "here" as we hurried back to "there"—until this year. It was during one of our more benevolent familial moments when we unanimously decided we would not do that marathon run. We all conceded that my husband and their father should not be required to spend two weeks completely exhausted.

That tends to happen to even the hardiest soul if two 1,000-mile treks bookend a week filled with French Canadian revelry.

The children and I began to have second thoughts and excused ourselves by wondering if the advantages of staying might not be outweighed by the disadvantages. After all, we had to tell Grandma and Grandpa. I had to tell my sisters. I had to tell my best friend.

Then there had been that close-to-Christmas experience when we had had our first Southern December. We had been in Spartanburg for about six months and, even though I walked every day, I had rarely seen anyone in our neighborhood. I began to wonder if I was living in a ghost town; until one evening, just before Christmas, looking out the window, I saw an eerie light in the sky reminiscent of the northern lights of home. I was drawn outside, hope filling my heart. But there were no northern lights. Only Christmas ones. Our street was lit up like Las Vegas. Sometime between the previous evening and this one, everyone on the street had put up Christmas lights. There were crêches, twinkling wreaths, and musical bells. When exactly had people put up all of those lights? Had everyone come out in the pitch of night in abeyance to some secret Southern ceremony and done their decorating? Why hadn't they invited me?

While my husband remained optimistic, I was determined to be a martyr, subtly trampling any good spirits that spilled over onto me. Spartanburg sided with my husband and was an admirable foe.

November brought the Dickens of a Christmas festival. Charles Dickens has long been one of my favorite authors, and I have always felt oddly connected to Victorian times. The choir, the Flagstar trees—the one in the plaza and the one in the office windows—the pipers, the living windows, and the hot chocolate which was more whipped cream than chocolate, melted the edges of my resolve. The pipers were probably the beginning of my undoing. But the couple (who, I am almost certain, had British accents) with the two little Scottie dogs were contributors also.

121

Canadians and Americans were born of the same mother. Canadians have never completely severed our British ties and have distanced ourselves rather more gently than our American siblings. (It has been said that Canadians expend most of their energy in dealing with the weather and hence have little left over for anything even remotely similar to a revolution.) To me, anything that even hints of Britain reeks of nostalgia, so walking down Main Street that evening might have weakened a lesser person's resolve, but no one was going to seduce me into enjoying a Christmas any different than the ones I had always been accustomed to. Still, my daughter coaxed me into getting out a few Christmas decorations to put up in the family room.

Then our neighbors invited us to the Christmas pageant at Morningside Baptist Church. The Hallelujah Chorus brought the congregation to its feet. My children said when it was all over, with awe, "Wow. That was pretty good." They were right, but it was hard for me to say so. We went home and began to put up decorations outside—some greenery and red plaid ribbons.

As Christmas drew near, my sister called to say that she and her children were flying down for the holidays. The little chink of light that had been chipped out by Dickens and Morningside Baptist brightened. That day we decorated the mailbox and the front step with holly from the shrubs near the house.

In speaking to a neighbor as he set up his crèche, (we were both in shirt sleeves), he said he felt he should be putting up Easter decorations instead. It occurred to me (but if ever asked, I will deny this) that spending a Christmas in warm weather, not having to worry about winter storms, might not be a bad thing. Big fat snowflakes sometimes were not big nor fat nor even snowflakes . . . they might be wind-driven pieces of ice that coated the roads and made you wonder if you would really even make it to Grandma's for Christmas dinner.

My sister arrived, and true to tradition, we went out with an ax and tried to find the perfect tree. Our luck was abysmal. At a tree grower, we found our tree. Contrary to widespread belief (mostly mine), it didn't matter that it was planted for this express purpose or that it was standing in a perfectly straight long line of clones, we still hollered "Timber!" and watched with immense satisfaction as it came tumbling down.

The following day we attended the Christmas concert at Bethlehem Baptist Church. There was that bustle of activity getting ready. The panic that often surfaces with too many people and not enough bathrooms never materialized. The children were intently discussing the Christmas carols they wanted most to hear. My husband recalled the man who used to sing at midnight Mass in Quebec—his astonishing voice when he sang Minuit Chretien. We were hoping that Mitch Crown, the choir director at Bethlehem and the only other person that we have ever encountered with a voice that matched the voice from those midnight services, would sing "O Holy Night." He didn't. But it didn't matter because he and his choir dissolved any lasting barriers that stood between me and a Christmas that I could feel was truly Christmas so far away from home and most of our family. That choir's voices lifted the rafters, turning the years back to Christmases of my past, rolling out the Christmases of the future before me. The golden thread that winds its way through each of our lives was still there. It had not unraveled, it had not drifted off in another direction. It was there, strengthened,

123

124

spun into the fabric of my family's life by all of the new Christmas traditions that had begun with our stay in the South and in Spartanburg for the holidays.

By the time we attended the candlelight Christmas Eve service at Second Presbyterian Church, my guard was down and I immersed myself fully in the joys of the season. All of the favorite hymns were there, all of the treasured rituals that linked me to our Canadian Christmas. The warm glow of the candles, the pews full of restless, eager children with the parents who were trying to make sure the church didn't catch on fire when all those candles were lit made everything right and good. Reverend Lassiter heightened the perfection by telling us just before we left that we should enjoy the full moon because it would be the last one mankind would see on a Christmas Eve for the next one hundred years.

And so it has begun, a new and perhaps not so different way to celebrate Christmas for our family here in Spartanburg. And some day, if we move back to our Canadian homeland, I know there will be Christmases where we will sit down in front of the fire on a brisk December night and say, "Remember the Dickens Christmas? Remember the times we went to Christmas Eve services and wore those light coats? Remember our tubs of holly that we cut from the trees at the front of our house? I really miss those things, don't you?"

Christmas in Spartanburg
1914

125

"Santa Claus:

I am a very smart little boy. I picked some cotton last fall. I want a French harp, a little automobile and some good things which you like best. And don't forget my two little brothers and don't forget Aunt Lettie. She is right smart."

Fred Berry

—From "Letters to Santa" printed in the Spartanburg Herald-Journal (1914).

FANNY WAS MY HOWLING MOTHER
By Rosa Shand

It was a blizzard and that was as it should be. Christmas wouldn't be just white, Christmas would stream ice—right off the spigot in the hotel room. Okay, the sorry hotel bed had foot-thick eiderdowns and okay there was warm tub water so we could make up powdered milk for the six-month-old and for the two-year-old. And yes, we found another human being, even arriving in the middle of the night like we did: a wet-capped red-cheeked woman breathed out fog in the downstairs hall and we could waylay her for questions.

"Of course, Love, we've heat in this country," says she. "Might try feeding your meter." "Feeding my what?" "Black box—on your wall there." "It wants what?" "Round metal bits, call them shillings over here." "Oh. So I give you dollars and you give me shillings?" "Sorry, Lovie, try down the street a piece." "I see the street's gone dark." "Some good soul turns up from time to time,

127

you'll see."

Some good soul turned up, time the sun came up. And no it wasn't Spartanburg. It was the London blizzard of 1961 and we—teacher husband, two babies, and I—were headed for Africa. By way of Benghazi, next stop over after London. And if you've never left a blizzard a few hours back, and in another middle of a Christmastime night stepped off a plane again, this time to a sweet warm breeze sloughing through date palms where you smell some drifting spice like maybe frankincense must smell and you made out a lighted arch in a low and earth-like building under stars that stun you—if you haven't done those things then you haven't been hit, all at once, in the dark, by the notion that you're standing at the spot it's all about, the place where the inn was full. And suddenly you feel it astonish-ing—that this is where you find yourself at Christmastime, walking in a warm sweet-smelling desert.

And then we were over the desert, looking down on an orange dawn that was glinting off the Nile. It was Christmas Eve, and we dropped down into Uganda, which was a blaze of yellow light and golden bougainvillea in between red roofs and flap-ping yellow-green trees. We found ourselves at a service of Lessons and Carols on a hilltop, Namirembe Cathedral. I'd never heard Lessons and Carols. I'd never had Christmas on a hilltop, in the sunshine, by banks of violet-petalled jacar-

128

anda trees and honey-smelling franjaponica trees and tangled vines of passionfruit, looking out on hills and the roofs of the city of Kampala. But that's where we were, and a tall slim princess of Buganda (she was actually draped in bright blue silk) was beside us, being pulled along by her children while she tried to smile and speak with us. She was happy. It showed in that sunshine, with "O Come All Ye Faithful" and the crowd of black and white and brown spilling out around her and behind her. It was exotic and it was Christmas. It was reassuring and it was strange.

We were staying in a flat on the grounds of Makerere College, the University of East Africa—a sister and brother-in-law had preceded us to the country, had taken us in with the Christmas tree, and we sat around a stunted-looking pine in the light of the summertime. The building was modern and the front wall of the room was glass, so we were flooded with sunlight. Then the dark dropped suddenly as it does on the equator I learned, without any warning of twilight, and all at once outside that wall of open glass there was a crowd of singers. Granted, our sense of time and place was slippery and hazy still, what with our quick surges over the globe and with the African altitude, but the welling up at once of dark and singing was as astounding as that warm breeze in the desert and that hill-top cathedral. The carolers were singing "O Little Town of Bethlehem." The night we'd left the

States different carolers had come to sing, and they had sung "O Little Town of Bethlehem" as well. But this was the other side of the world. I'd loved singing at Christmastime, so I knew this carol was written by a man named Phillips Brooks who'd studied where we'd studied, in Virginia. That seemed a powerful connection in this odd Christmas place. But here Brooks' words were sung by Ugandans, and to a quite strange English tune.

Christmas dinnertime the house was filled with foot-loose homesick strangers, who'd come from far-off countries like America. One was a Southern black, a woman named Fanny Bird. Now I'd been living away from my South Carolina home for years, in Virginia and in Washington, and we'd been traveling a week in England and Uganda and it had been a very long time since I'd heard Southern speech. But suddenly I head my mother speaking. I spun around. It wasn't my mother, it was Fanny Bird. She was telling a story the very same way my mother told a story. She didn't sound like other English-speaking people I'd halfway gotten used to, who talked ideas and information. Fanny was entertaining us, Southern fashion, laughing with that howl I knew so well, using her hands in that mocking way I knew so intimately because it was my mother's howling laugh and peculiar turn of her hands. I hadn't heard it in years, not outside my Carolina, but now I was hearing it. Every intonation. It set off my own howl of a laugh. I was at

130

home, and reassured, and dizzily confused.

My mother was a Southern white woman. My mother assumed the separation from the blacks she lived among—it was only 1961. My mother (and myself), we knew we had a different culture from the blacks we were tangled with. We knew we spoke a different language. After all, a pretty huge ruckus had been boiling up for a couple of centuries or so about precisely those supposedly catastrophic differences. But here, at this sunny Christmas dinner in Uganda, I was back in South Carolina. I was listening to my mother.

My mother and Fanny Bird would never know each other. But they had absorbed and become one another, and neither of them suspected it. You had to be in a changed state of mind, and maybe five thousand miles away among foreigners at Christmastime before you saw this thing, this oneness of the South—this South that was shouting its differences out to the world.

The sounds and smells and colors of that Christmastime were dizzily intense, the familiar mixed with the strange. Of course that too-odd heightening of things can't come again like that. But we squirrel up morsels, most probably from childhood, so that Christmas air in Spartanburg swarms with sweet past Christmases—in Uganda or Columbia or Pacolet. But arteries harden, and Christmastime in cities brings on suicides. The ones who can't root up some friends—or who have

131

beaten friends and family off—are cursed by the same rich memories, which—from outside lighted windows—twist themselves knifesharp. It's the best of times and the worst of times. It's hope larded through with haunted loneliness. Yet it could be it's in that heightened state that insights come most readily—the way I happened, that Christmas Day in East Africa, to see what everybody all my life had kept so well concealed—that glowing manifestation, over Christmas dinner in Uganda, of the oneness of our Southern being.

Christmas in Tucapau
1914

133

"Dear Santa Claus

      I live at Tucapau. I am eight years old and go to school every day. Please bring me lots of good things to eat and some firecrackers and some gloves for me and my sister Jeannette to wear to school. Old Santa, I have four goats and you must come to see me and I will give you a ride. Will close."

Fay Elder

*—From "Letters to Santa" printed in the Spartanburg
Herald-Journal (1914).*

Decorating the Tree
By Matthew Teague

nytime anyone asks me about Christmas I remember the one Christmas party I had. It was when I lived in Spartanburg at this great Depression-era house on Lucas Court. Besides the dorms, it was the first unparented place I'd lived, and I had this noble sense of staking claim to my life—having a yard and a dog and all that. I was living there with my old pal Tyler and we were both finishing up school that year. Tyler was this dark creature who lived with loud music, reading magazines under a dangle dim light in his bedroom. I was whatever I was at that age—distraught by God or love or whatever melodramatic humbug I could concoct in my head. So we lived like we lived, and then about eight o'clock every night we'd pull up the bootstraps and get blind drunk as a sort of last resort at a good time. It usually worked. We're still truest friends.

We had gotten on some big kick about entertaining then, throwing parties and making slightly better than college-style hors d'oeuvres. I still get on those image kicks sometimes. I recently read how Frank Sinatra and Dean Martin drank their Manhattans, and I tried to emulate it as best I could, for three days. But as much as I love Manhattans, I always wind up back with Budweiser.

So it was Christmas and I already had that whole sense of place thing going at the house. But it felt like home—really and truly home—only after I dragged a Christmas tree through the front door. I got it up in the stand and we had an idea for decorating the thing. Entertaining—it seemed what we should do.

Tyler and I wrote up what we thought were incredibly inspired invitations and mailed them out. Come to think of it, there was a Sinatra quotation in there somewhere, but I don't recall what it was. We sent them to all our friends and all those we wanted to know better, people like Shay with her good red hair.

The party was scheduled for Friday, and on the Saturday before I had a date. It was one of the few actual *first dates* I'd been on—usually something sleazy just turned less so, or some old friend and I eventually fell into bed. But this was a date. Elizabeth. I cooked for her and we went to see *A River Runs Through It*. I remember that she cried when the two brothers got in a fight and their mother got knocked to the floor. That impressed me. We had quiet gin and scotch at a table by The Peddler's dark wooden bar and walked all over Spartanburg's gray downtown that night. It was a cold December and we huddled in coats. She told me about her parents and they sounded like mine. She was sweet and beautiful and thoroughly kind. Tall, so it was like I was looking up at the sky when I kissed her goodnight.

Then the next night, Sunday, I wound up down at the fraternity house. Lila was there—all short and trim and cropped blond hair, and she painted, which melts me some. She said she'd split with her boyfriend a few weeks earlier. We went on for hours talking about our whole lives. She'd been abused when she was a little girl—horrible stories it would do no good to repeat—and that made me feel for her. And God she was gorgeous and somehow well . . .

137

But I'd just had the date with Elizabeth. The sweet one from the movie. I made myself forget about her.

Friday afternoon I was standing on the front porch gathering the rubbish that had accumulated and sweeping before the party that night. The sun was starting to fall when Elizabeth came by with an ornament, apologizing that she had to go out of town that night. She said that she wasn't mad but that she knew about Lila, gave me a hug and the softest saddest kiss I've ever had. She handed me the box, white with gold ribbon tied on it like she'd gone to some trouble, and drove away in her silver truck. I stood there in the yard just watching as she went down the road, and I didn't move for some time. She gave me a faultless ornament of mirrors, creased and spinning and sending off cracked light. I took it inside and hung it from the tree and tried to watch it as it turned.

Tyler and I cleaned inside the house and had the party set to go. Lila came over and brought wind chimes. They didn't even hang on the tree like they were supposed to, but I'd fallen by then and they seemed perfect. And though I remember little of the Christmas party, I know that it was one of the best times I've ever had.

138

For the next three weeks or so Lila and I were near-inseparable. Like always, it was completely overpowering. I don't know how it happened. And I can't explain what happened over Christmas break—she went a little crazy like women can, just after I'd decided that I was completely and totally in love with her. I was twenty. It doesn't take much then, maybe ever.

After Christmas I spent little time talking to either Lila or Elizabeth. Lila broke my heart and somehow with Elizabeth I managed to break my own.

When I think of Christmas, when I think of the party and the time on Lucas Court, I have to think carefully to remember it all—Lila, Elizabeth, even the tree. But another friend brought over a small piece of board that she'd hung on twine as an ornament for the tree—its image is always readily at hand. She painted this faded Jesus on one side and this faded Devil on the other. It just spun there on a limb while everyone drank and had fun. It's in storage back in South Carolina, and each Christmas I put up a tree and miss it. I never think to get it when I am home, but I need it all year long. ⚲

GRANDDADDY'S SONG

By Gary Henderson

My granddaddy's talent for growing dahlias, chrysanthemums, and roses was always better than his singing, but that never stopped him from raising his voice in song, especially when he was tilling the plants in his garden. Most of the songs were the timeworn hymns of his faith, but others were relics of his childhood. And the Christmas Eve when he sang one of them thirty-one years ago, is a moment I'll never forget. In places far away, I've used the memory many times in late December to bring me home to Spartanburg on Christmas Eve.

141

My family gathered each Christmas Eve to exchange gifts and have supper. This event was held at my aunt Dorothy and uncle Nolen's house, a neat bungalow on Spartanburg's north side. Aunt Dot was my mother's only sister. By late afternoon, my uncles, aunts, cousins, and grandparents would fill the house with laughter and warm conversation. The gifts would be stacked under the tree and the dining room table covered with food. These were the times when our family seemed closest.

For my Granddaddy, John M. Johnson—my grandmother called him Johnny—these Christmas Eve celebrations were the finest moments of his life. Granddaddy came to all of these Christmas gatherings dressed in a navy blue suit, starched white dress shirt, and necktie. And my grandmother, Lillie Belle, whom we called Mamma Johnson, joined him by wearing one of her "Sunday dresses" for the occasions.

I've always thought I knew Granddaddy better than his six other grandchildren because my mother and I lived with him and my grandmother while my dad was a soldier, and away at war. Throughout his life, I was close to him. He was the one who taught me to drive a car when I was still only eleven. He sat with me in church on Sundays, only used swear words when he got real mad, and sometimes sang to me.

"I never got much for Christmas when I was a boy," Granddaddy used to tell me, not looking for pity. He just wanted me to appreciate the things I was fortunate enough to have. Not that my family was rich. We weren't even close to it. "The most I could look for was a few pieces of fruit and maybe a little candy," Granddaddy would continue. "Some years Santa Claus didn't even stop at our house."

Granddaddy was born in the Clifton Mill village in 1894. Both his parents died within months after he was born, and he was reared by relatives. He was already working in the mill by the time he was eight years old, and on his own by the time he was in his early teens. Although many decades had passed, the memories of childhood haunted him, especially around Christmas. I think that's why he and my grandmother always spent more than they could afford on their grandchildren.

I remember only a few of the many Christmas gifts Granddaddy and Mama Johnson gave me. One of them—an expensive windup car Granddaddy bought on credit at Skelton's Toy Store on Main Street when I was ten—was passed on to my son. Dented and dusty, it sits on a book shelf in his home in Charleston, a treasure from a great-grandfather he never knew.

But the gift I value most is the last one he gave me—the memory of my Granddaddy's Christmas song. It wasn't wrapped in pretty paper and ribbons, but I believe Granddaddy knew the gift would someday be a treasure.

"Let's sing some Christmas carols," someone suggested one year as everyone returned to the living room after our Christmas supper. Our family often sang a couple of carols at these gatherings, and someone—usually one of the grandchildren— read the Christmas story from the Bible.

"Daddy, do you remember how you used to

143

144

sing for us?" my aunt Dot asked. "Yeah, Grand-daddy, sing for us," a child's voice begged. Each of his three children—my mother, Lois, her brother, John, and her sister, Dorothy—and all seven of his grandchildren had known the joy of his singing. But on this night, none of us really expected him to sing. Heart disease had slowed his steps and made him weak. His slightly rotund body had become thin and he was pale. He used a cane to walk and small strokes had slurred his speech.

"We've been to Christmas trees all over town, with lots of girls and boys . . . " Granddaddy sang in perfect pitch. His voice was strong, and he sang the words clearer than we had heard him speak in a long time. For a few moments, it seemed his heart lifted free of illness. Other voices in the room stopped. Everyone turned toward where Grand-daddy sat in a wing back chair near the Christmas tree. It had been years since the last time any of us had heard him sing. But we remembered other Christmases when his song was part of our celebra-tion. As Granddaddy sang, he leaned forward and balanced himself on his black cane. He sang every verse of the song, without forgetting a word.

As Granddaddy finished singing, tears filled his deep-blue eyes. We applauded like we had heard the performance of our lifetime. And we probably had.

When he finished singing, Granddaddy pulled out his handkerchief, dried his eyes, and learned back in his chair. We didn't sing any other Christmas carols that year.

After the party was over, I drove Granddaddy and Mama Johnson home and helped them get inside. The gray skies of the afternoon had darkened and it felt like snow might fall. In the house, it was warm, still, and silent. After I unloaded the gifts that they'd received, I wished them a Merry Christmas and told them good night.

That Christmas Eve was the last time our entire family was together for a holiday. Less than two months after my Granddaddy sang, he suffered a severe stroke early one Sunday morning. He died a week later on Valentine's Day.

The memory of that Christmas Eve family gathering in Spartanburg will never fade. It wouldn't seem like the holidays without it. Rarely has a song about Christmas trees been sung so well. And never with as much heart.

145

"I'll never forget that Christmas," my aunt Dorothy, who is nearing seventy years old, said to me recently. "Daddy sang that little song to all of us when we were growing up, and then to all you grandchildren, too. I never knew where he learned it."

Neither did I. I've looked through libraries and in every old song book I've come across, but I've never found the song. And the first line of the first verse is all I can remember. Even so, the song about the Christmas trees will always be part of my holidays. I'll sing the one line I know and whistle the rest of it. I'm always hoping for another Christmas miracle, but if I never find the words in a book, that's all right, too. Because for me, it will always be Granddaddy's Song.

Christmas in Campobello
Early 1920s

147

"Oranges were a very special luxury to us, something just
for the Christmas season. Items of clothing were another
regular feature. These usually would have had to be bought for
us at some time during the winter in any event, but when given at
Christmas, they made the collection of gifts look larger. These
could be a handkerchief ... shoe laces, a cap for a boy, a hat for
a girl, a coin purse, underclothes or another useful item."

—*From "Our Way of Life: The Odyssey of a Farm Family" by
Ryan A. Page (1982).*

21

FULL MOON AND LIGHTS
By Elaine Lang Ferguson

The phone rings. Our ten-year-old niece Alexsis has asked her dad to call. She wants to know when Uncle Michael is going to take her around town to look at Christmas lights. Every year we drive the country and curvy neighborhood roads of Spartanburg, searching for spectacular displays of light and goodwill. Michael smiles into the mouthpiece; his blue eyes are sparkling. "How about six o'clock tomorrow?" he asks. His tenderness touches me. "He really is a great uncle," I think. A wave of emotion and ancient desire wells up in me and I pray for pregnancy.

Incredibly, I realize it is already the day before Christmas. I am thankful for the rituals we have established with our family and friends. Decorating the Christmas tree is a major ritual. This year, we decorated the tree two days before I had surgery. Michael made a fire, then pulled down the rickety attic steps and ascended. He passed down the boxes filled with treasure. I unpacked while Alvin and the Chipmunks sang Christmas carols. They're midwives to the child within me (Michael is less than fond of them). Within a few minutes, I find the creamy colored paper angel. She has a garland-like halo of dried red roses and gold glitter. She signified hope for me.

I place the angel at the top of the tree. Then I uncover two more angels; these are made from corn husks, with flowing garments and heart shaped wings. Each carries a delicate flower bouquet, one burgundy and the other turquoise. They're a gift from our boss Shirley. Every year she gives hand-made ornaments crafted by her sister. A couple of little clothespin and felt ornaments fashioned by me and my sister Liz follow—a little drummer boy and a clown. Michael puts on a disc by the Chieftans now. He loves the energy of their Irish music and begins to fiddle as I unpack memories.

Growing up, we used to make some type of ornament every year with my Mom. She and my sister Liz painted the plaster Santa and Mrs. Claus that I hang next. There's a gingerbread Santa from our niece Jennifer, and red and green felt ornaments from Ali and Lawson, whose Mom taught them to sew the year before last. I try each ornament in one spot, then another, until its proper place is found. My husband looks on with an amused grin.

As I handle a pair of crocheted white ice skates with paperclip blades, I see my Mother making them just a few years ago. I remember how she used to crochet all the sweaters, coats, and hats for our Barbie dolls. I am amazed how she could work, cook and clean house, and still find time to make toys. I realize that love sewed those tiny blouse buttons; love fluffed the furry hat rims. And love glued shiny blue stars all along the lace holes of these skates.

Later in the afternoon, we plan to go to midnight Mass with my little sister and her husband. It's a mandatory and sacred ritual, a piece of childhood brought to life by a quick car drive. When we enter St. Paul's for Mass, I think of Michael's mother. This church was packed with people during her funeral, a community affected by and appreciative of her artistic gifts. We have her rosaries set out around our house. They are portals for prayer, a connection to our ancient past.

I often carry a rosary with me when I leave the house. Tonight I have a crystal topaz rosary, with beads that sparkle in the candlelight from the altar. I remember buying it from an earthy woman in Prague, outside a beautiful cathedral. I carry it in a butter-colored leather pouch, purchased from a ladysmith at Covent Garden. As the celebration begins, I concentrate on singing every verse in the Christmas carol. Afterwards, we exchange greetings with several friends. Mary laughs and introduces us to her brother. Andreas shakes Michael's

151

hand and I give him a big hug. Trish, Allen and John Edgerton exchange hugs and kisses with us. We all play soccer on Sunday afternoons out at the 295 fields. We are thankful for our circle of friends, for the pattern of community we weave.

We usually spend Christmas day alone. When we wake, one of us puts on John Lennon's "Happy Christmas (War is Over)." As song fills the room, we kiss and gently nuzzle each other. We light a fire. Then we touch here, and we touch there, beginning to make love slowly as the Christmas tree lights twinkle. This year my folks have stayed three weeks to help us out after the surgery. They slept head to head with us, separated only by a thin wall. We did not enjoy our usual Christmas ritual. Yet I liked having them stay with us awhile.

On Christmas morning, we play music for my family as we embark on festivities. We eat pancakes to Leon Redbone and open presents to the Modern Mandolin Quartet's Nutcracker Suite. I realize that the Nativity scene has still not been set out. I remember fighting once, as a child, with my brother John over who would arrange the pieces in the beautiful Nativity scene Mom made. As I carry my white figurines out to the flower box by the front door, I notice purple and yellow pansies blooming. They smile with me in celebration of the season, as I wistfully wish for snow. I want to ride the hilly land here. I want to warm myself by the neighborhood bonfire atop the large hill at Dairy

Ridge Road. Last year Michael and I took some of the small hills on cafeteria trays. We'd been inspired by Luanne's accounts of Wofford students on the Memorial Auditorium hill. This year we have cool new sleds, and we mean to try out the big hill. I am ready for the excitement and the peacefulness snow will bring.

Once it's dark, we pick up Alexsis. We head out past the Kohler plant and drive for quite awhile before turning left. Eventually, we see the little Christmas Lights sign staked near the highway. Michael quickly turns right and we wind down a country road. We drive a good distance before we pass a small house, with a single strand of colored lights twinkling from the rail of its tiny porch. What seems like miles later, we see another solitary house with an evergreen tree in its front yard decorated with green lights. We begin to wonder just where the sign will lead. We sing Christmas carols and look around expectantly.

153

Suddenly, we all point at once, "Up there, on the left." The flow of lights permeates the night sky. A whole community of lighted animals and people radiates. It's like the town of Whoville, where the Grinch could not steal Christmas. Celebrating the birth of hope and love are Santas, snowmen, and soldiers; nutcrackers, reindeer, carolers, and choir boys; Jesus, Mary, and Joseph. Angels look on lovingly here and there, and a large friendly snowman in the center tips his hat and waves to us. We smile and laugh, our eyes are bright with excitement. We marvel at the wonder of the scene.

We tear ourselves away and continue our quest to find an even more spectacular display. Our travels take us past our own home. Underneath the cedars and huge evergreen are two little reindeer, twinkling in the dark. They are snowy white light and metal sculptures with tiny red noses. One is grazing, nose next to the earth. The other is looking up ready to leap into the sky with Santa. They are charming, and I am full of joy. Alexsis comically begins to rate the light displays. She gives our reindeer a very poor rating. I pretend to pout. Michael grins and drives toward our old Linville Hills neighborhood.

As we drive off and pass the Deaf and Blind School, we all notice the moon, large and luminous in the black blanket of sky. Clouds swirl in front of the moon, and I am in awe of Creation. I breathe in the beauty. "I'll give it a five," Alexsis says. (One is the highest score, and seven the lowest so far in her rating system.) "I'm going to tell God!"

We ride by the old drag strip and see a well-lighted fountain spraying water, in front of a two-story mansion. The porch and balcony are decorated with evergreen garland and gold bows. Every window has a candle burning, as if tiny children peek out to catch sight of Santa in his sleigh, and five reindeer prepare the sleigh, just around the side

154

of the house. Alexsis is gleeful. She wants to give this a one! Michael asks Alexsis to reconsider, as we drive toward Reidville Road; he doesn't see how anything can outrank the first scene.

When we reach our old neighborhood, it feels a little like heaven and a little bit like Las Vegas. Practically every yard is decorated with colorful and completely absorbing displays of light. One family has a large, beautifully colored Nativity scene. Mary has on a blue veil, and the Wise Men are wearing gorgeous red, green, and purple robes. There are donkeys and sheep, angels and stars and bells. All the bushes glow colored lights. And the trees are transformed into Shakers, reaching out to the Heavens in a trance dance. We spend a long, long time there. We inspect each street and each individual yard scene. We encounter display after display of dazzling red, green, and white lights; Santas, snowmen, stars, and nutcrackers. Each one reflects the joy and creativity of the householder. We bask in the glow of the twinkling lights, and the glow of Good Will. Alexsis sums up the experience later, at our traditional Boxing Day breakfast. Over kippers, tea, and toast, she announces quite pensively, yet smiling broadly, "I really loved the Christmas lights. And even though it didn't snow, we had the full moon."

155

22

CHRISTMAS COTTON

By Mike Hembree

The cotton. That's what's missing from Christmas.

The fruit of snow-white fields fueled and fed Spartanburg County for many years, creating jobs for thousands, fortunes for a few and a way of life for generations. A son of textile workers growing up at a time of profound change in the cotton-mill industry, I had only superficial connections with the fiber that would provide my family's first automobile and fund much of my education. Yet, on one Christmas in the 1950s, cotton became a wreath of winter for me, and a sign of time to come.

In the late nineteenth century, textile villages grew up in rings around the city of Spartanburg, or "town," as those of us beyond the last suburbs called it, then as now. Mills, then dams, then bridges, then houses, then schools and churches were built. At Glendale, at Pacolet, at

157

Clifton, the land and the people were transformed. The workers who stepped though the doors of the mill walked into more than a job. They became virtual children of cotton, with practically every aspect of their lives linked to the mills.

For decades, it was generally assumed that sons would follow fathers into the deafening whir of the mills, and it was the young married couple's dream to move into a mill house of their own, if only down the narrow, winding street from Ma and Pa. The mill village was its own universe.

Part of the mill-hill mindset began to dissolve in the middle years of the century, however, driven by forces within and without. There was strenuous competition for the textile dollar, and South Carolina factories faced threats both foreign and domestic. The relative comforts of the insular mill village were no longer taken for granted, and the very heart of the paternalistic nature of the system began to change. The houses that mill companies had rented to workers were sold, usually to the workers living in them (a purchase that became a landmark moment in many mill families' lives). In the Clifton and Converse mill villages operated by the Clifton Manufacturing Company on the eastern edge of Spartanburg County, this sweeping event occurred in the otherwise Eisenhower-quiet of the 1950s, opening the door to bedrock changes that would shake the communities in the two decades to come. Ultimately, the mills would close, forcing societal and economic movement that, to some, was devastating.

As a kid growing up near the Clifton mill villages in the 1950s, I had no hint of the potential reach of the changes that were coming. Free to roam the hills and woods of the area, oblivious to the concerns our parents might have brought home from the weaving room or the card room, my friends and I romped on the same river banks mill-hill kids had explored since the late 1800s. On Saturdays, we went to town with our parents, visited the toy counters at Woolworth's and Silver's, ate hot doughnuts at Zimmerman's and saw a movie at the Palmetto.

The constants in our lives were home, school, church, and the mill shift schedule.

And the trucks. Big flatbed trucks owned by the company lumbered over the village roads at all hours, hauling cotton bales and cotton products from one mill to another, up and down the river.

The trucks also gave me a Christmas.

As they traveled, the wind carried small scrap pieces of cotton from the flatbeds to the sides of the road, where they clung to bushes and weeds, becoming inadvertent decorative objects. By the age of eight, I had decided that the Christmas tree we brought into our house each December wasn't enough, so I wandered into the small patch of woods down the hill behind the house in search of a small tree I could adopt for the season. I found a small, scraggly, orphaned cedar at the edge of a ravine (it was a ravine then; now I see it as simply a gully). I hung three of four Christmas balls I had pirated from the house and tossed a few silver icicles. The crowning touch, though, was the cotton picked from the side of the road and draped around the now-struggling branches of the little cedar.

The mill company, the big sugar daddy for all of us, everyone, had made my Christmas tree. It was nice, I remember thinking, as pretty as one of those trees in the Christmas dioramas at Aug. W. Smith's in town.

The wind blew with a hint of snow. I sat back and admired my handiwork and imagined all the forest creatures coming to visit my tree in the light and cold of the December moon.

I hadn't thought about that tree until almost thirty years later, in December of 1986, when I was preparing a Christmas program for church and, in the process, interviewed some of the community's older residents about Christmas in "the old days." Among them was Sallie Cash, whose family had moved to Clifton from the North Carolina mountain foothills in 1904. Three days after their arrival, the father and five of the family's six children, including Sallie, then eleven, went to work in the mill at Clifton No. 1.

Not long after the family settled in a village mill house, father and mother and children attended a Christmas service at Clifton First Baptist Church.

The memory Sallie carried from that Christmas Eve night was the sight of her first Christmas tree, lit by candles in the sanctuary of a small wooden church, high on a hill above the Pacolet River.

"Of course, it was old times and they didn't have the Christmas tree all decorated up like they do now," she said, her eyes sparkling at a memory eight decades old. "It was just a plain cedar tree with little candles stuck around over it." The family left church that night without presents, for only those children whose parents had brought gifts to put under the tree went home with one.

I had not thought about my forest cotton tree in all the intervening years, but Sallie's story made me wonder if it had survived all the Christmases between. Her tree and mine were less than a mile (though generations) apart. On a trip home later that winter, I climbed through the underbrush and found what must have been the tree, still guarding the ravine, still tattered and ragged, but now almost twenty feet tall. My eyes got teary. Perhaps at childhood lost, or maybe it was the wind.

Now Christmas comes to a silent mill town. The old riverside factories that once jumped with activity and were cores for all that happened in the communities are virtually lifeless, serving largely as warehouses or pigeon roosts. Only the river, rolling on toward Pacolet, the fall line and the Atlantic, is much the same. The paternalism of the mill fathers and the mill system left when the heart of

161

the mighty factories stopped. The change was felt even in matters as seemingly trivial but as traditionally emotional as the giving of fruit and candy bags at Christmas, long a practice at many mill village churches and one that was supported for many years by donations from the company.

Gone now, for years.

So, too, are the flatbed trucks, no longer a daily presence on Coopertown Road and River Street. And, on the side of the road, there is no cotton, blowing in the wind.

162

Christmas in Campobello
Early 1920s

163

"A week or two before Christmas, Papa and Mama would ride off to town, leaving the rest at home. They would return late in the afternoon, shooing all of us away from the buggy."

—From "Our Way of Life: The Odyssey of a Farm Family"
by Ryan A. Page (1982).

23.

CHRISTMAS LETTER: 1996

by Meg Barnhouse

Dear Friends and Family,

It has been warm weather here in Spartanburg for most of the month, so it is when we visit the new mall that we feel Christmas the most. Before the big renovations I used to gasp for air after twenty minutes in the place. It felt like a mausoleum. A mausoleum with jewelry stores. The new mall has long skylights in the ceilings, so now I can breathe in there more easily.

I used to avoid the mall at all costs, and I prided myself on breaking the record of number of months between visits. Eleven months, I think, was my all-time record. What I like to do instead is to wake up at five o'clock one November morning and order everything on the Christmas list from catalogs with all-night numbers. It feels like getting away with something, shopping in my bathrobe, sipping coffee, never having to look at a shoe store. Shoe stores make me surly. It comes from having big feet as a girl in the era of Cinderella. She was sweet-tempered, hard-working, and had tiny feet. On my best days I only got one out of three.

This year I went to the new mall four or five times during November and December. The first couple of times I had to follow my ten-year-old around. He seemed to grasp the new layout with no effort. He's almost always right, at ten, about the "where" of things. I'm still better at the "why" and, of course, the "how much."

At one of the entrances to the mall there is a huge talking reindeer. More accurately, it is a reindeer head stuck on a body made out of a brown plush bag. Its mouth opens and shuts while its head moves back and forth like a politician's. Its voice is low and blurred. We can't make out the words, but they sound sinister. My two boys decided last night to pretend the stuffed reindeer was possessed, and they give him a wide berth, sliding their bodies along the walls to go around him and calling to each other, "Don't look him in the eye, he'll get you!" They pretend the same thing about the Santa Clauses hired for the season. I don't reprimand them. The reindeer is creepy, and Santa *is* an anagram for Satan after all. I heard that from a preacher on the radio.

That possessed reindeer down at the new mall reminds me that we all lose our minds at

166

Christmas, reaching for something grand and stirring. Christmas inspires us to let go of the common sense by which we normally protect ourselves from being ridiculous. In Spartanburg, over the years, I have seen evidence of this. There is the family who has an American flag in their yard made of Christmas lights. There is the yard with a statue of Jesus with his toenails painted red, surrounded by Santa and the seven dwarfs. There was a billboard on Pine Street I remember from the eighties that showed a lovely portrait of the Holy Family with the words underneath: "Merry Christmas from Thompson's Exterminators."

This year a downtown church is offering, as their gift to the community, a drive-through nativity pageant where five hundred members of their congregation plus live animals act out the Christmas story for "pilgrims" driving by. I want to take my children to see that this afternoon. They had a wonderful time the year our next-door neighbors put on a live nativity pageant in their front yard. I'm looking forward to being a drive-by pilgrim. As a collector of odd experiences, I know when you combine live animals with a flock of church people doing something spiritual, the potential for oddity is strong and mighty.

The most bizarre thing I saw this year was on television, where someone at VH-1 had unearthed a clip of David Bowie singing "Little Drummer Boy" with Bing Crosby. You tell me what drug

167

the record company exec was on to have said, "Hey! We'll get Bing Crosby to sing 'Little Drummer Boy!' And who would be perfect to sing it with him? I know— David Bowie!" What I saw was Bing looking disgusted, like he is singing a duet with a tarantula. He won't make eye contact with Bowie or even glance in his general direction. His face says he is a pro, but by golly he is going to get this Little Drummer thing OVER with and take Mary out for lunch and a few Old Fashioneds. Bowie begins the song looking like he too would rather be anywhere else, but by the second verse he is enjoying Bing's disapproval. I could almost see him visualizing himself as a big old bisexual rock and roll spider, preening in the face of Bing Crosbyness and all it stands for. If it is possible to make "The Little Drummer Boy" sound corrupt, Bowie did it.

168

I lost my mind and became ridiculous this Christmas too. I hate to tell that, but it's true. I tried to be an entrepreneur, which has never before worked in my life. I got a tip about a shipment of Nintendo 64s, a toy my sons wanted with a glittering fervor. I seized the day and bought two, thinking I would sell one through the paper and make some extra money for presents. It was a miserable failure. I felt guilty selling something for more than I'd paid. Somehow my conscience is not comfortable with that basic business concept. After trying to deal on the phone with the shady-sounding man named Tony who answered my ad, I ended up taking the cursed thing back to the store yesterday and getting my money back. They cheered.

I'm hoping this year you all are not immune to making yourselves ridiculous in the engaging pandemonium of the season. I hope you all have given too much, loved too much, eaten too much and thrown yourselves into all the celebrations of the return of the light into dark winter. You all are lights in my life, and I plan to be a light in yours. All blessings to you, and may your common sense return after it's had a good vacation.

—Meg

169

24

LOOKING FOR THE MAGIC

By Georgie Dickerson

171

My grandfather was a carpenter and building contractor. The large gray house he built for his family shines in my memory like a diamond in a setting of large pecan trees. Frank, the dog Granddaddy said he bought for a dollar and a duck, lived in the fenced back yard. The house was located at the corner of Irby and Chamblin Streets in Woodruff. Although there was a city water supply, Granddaddy kept the well and the hand-well pump on the back porch. I loved to pump the sweetest, coldest water in town and hear the spilled water drop back into the well with an echoing splash. It was almost like magic.

I have always looked for the magic in my life and in the lives of those around me. Looking for the magic began around Christmas time when I was a little girl; the magic of Santa Claus, the jolly old man who would fill my life and my stocking with just the things I wanted, and the magic of a grand-father who loved me best.

I was looking for the magic the day I was allowed to help make Christmas mints in my grandma's green kitchen. The walls, the trim around the windows, and even the doors were painted a pale green. The ceiling was so high it hurt my neck to look up. The light bulb hung from a long cord in the center of the room. Granddaddy had built cabinets and counters along the back wall, so the kitchen looked modern, but Grandma still used a wood stove for cooking in the winter months. We could always find crickets in the wood box, warming themselves by the stove.

The mouth of the stove was red and blazing when Grandma clanked the iron door open to push in wood, and the heat blasted us when we got too close. Spit sizzled and popped on the surface of the stove when Grandma tested the heat. The magical mint-making began when Grandma mea-sured sugar, water, and butter into a large pot and set it on the stove to cook. The boiling mint mix-ture occasionally popped out on the stove top and the smell of burnt sugar mingled with the faint odor of burning wood.

Making mints today requires a slab of marble that is chilled in the freezer to pour the mints on and chill them quickly, but Grandma used her large cast-iron sink that had all its pipes showing. Cousin Frances and I were given the job of washing the sink. We stood on chairs and scrubbed and scrubbed; we thought it was clean, but Grandma scrubbed it one more time. Granddaddy took a chunk of ice from the ice box, wrapped it in a towel and squatted down and held it under the sink bottom; more ice was put in the sink. I tried to help him hold the ice but it was too heavy and cold for my hands. The cold sink had to be buttered so the mint mixture would not stick.

After testing the liquid mints until she was satisfied that they were ready for the sink, Grandma shooed us away and carefully picked up the pot with several layers of cloths, carried it across the room and poured it in the clean cold sink. I looked at the still boiling smoking bubbling stuff sizzling in the sink and could not imagine how this could turn into mints. It had to be magic.

173

We buttered our hands and tried to smear each other with the greasy stuff while we waited until the mints cooled enough to touch. Grandma and Granddaddy began handling the mixture carefully. It slid around on their buttered hands and lopped over the sides, but they kept working it with their hands and started to pull it back and forth, twisting each time they pulled. Finally cousin Frances and I were given our mints to pull. It was still so hot we almost dropped it on the floor, but we kept moving it around and began to pull it. I backed across the kitchen pulling the mints and then Frances folded the mints and came back to me. One time we had a rope so long that it almost fell on the floor. We hoped that our grandparents did not see those dirty smudges our hands were leaving on the mints.

The mints were getting more firm, and it was time to add the peppermint flavoring and the food coloring. We laid the mints down on the counter and Grandma divided them into two piles. She poured a little green food coloring in one blob and red in the other. A little flavoring was added to each also. Frances and I mixed in the green coloring, we mashed and folded the mints till the color was evenly distributed. I wanted to help mix the red coloring too, but my hands were green and the two colors would blend and make muddy-looking mints instead of pretty pale pink and green ones.

174

We began twisting the mints into little long ropes and laid them in rows on the counter. I was tired and wanted to quit, but mints were not magic, they required hard persistent work.

We put waxed paper in the mint tins and watched Grandma cut the long ropes of candy into little pillow shapes with her kitchen scissors. Finally the mints were finished and it was tasting time. I bit into the candy and was surprised and disappointed. The peppermint was so strong it took away the sweet taste. I spit it out of my mouth and threw it in the garbage. The mints were surely not magic tasting! I could not understand how the grownups could eat those strong mints. My cousin bragged about how good the mints tasted, but I noticed she went to the well pump and got a glass of cold water.

Enjoy
nancy Ogle

25.

MAGGIE
By Nancy Jenkins Ogle

177

From the side window of my house I often watch the children as they play. They are a rough and tumble lot, making up their games at will. The rules are never the same; each child improvises and expects the others to follow. The mop becomes a horse, bare feet pound the dusty yard. Cowboys and Indians shoot it out from behind the trees and around the fence. Wrapped in an old tattered blanket, a cat thinly disguised as a baby snarls and scratches at its would-be mother. Dressed in a long dress, patiently teaching the 3Rs to two big brothers and a goat, a little girl becomes the school teacher for the day. The din and laughter echo through my closed doors and windows. Only the dead of winter will drive the children inside.

They are the Owens children. All are blond or have light brown hair, eyes the color of chestnuts. They are neat, clean, bright, and picture pretty. The daddy is a police officer, the mother a tired and harried housewife. There are too many mouths to feed on one salary. Nestled near the bottom rung of this stair-step brood is Maggie. She is no more than four years old. A close look reveals a thin, tanned girl wearing clothing a size too large or too small. She will give me a shy smile but never a word. I know her voice from the sound of her at play. She has become a favorite of mine.

Around Thanksgiving the games begin to take on a Christmas theme. Maggie gives up her school teacher's role to become an angel. Wise Men on a make-believe camel wind their way past my window. "Santa's gonna bring me a . . . " becomes the topic of conversation. I eavesdrop and worry; Santa will certainly need some help.

It was near midnight on Christmas Eve. I heard several muffled sounds and saw Maggie's uncle and oldest siblings assembling a swing and slide set in the play yard. The weather was bitter cold and a feel of snow was in the air. My heart filled with joy and relief. Santa Claus has found the Owens children. To bed, to sleep, all is right with the world.

Maggie's voice awakens me from a sound sleep. A quick look at my bedside clock. Why, it is 4 a.m. I must have been dreaming. There it is again: peals of laughter, squeals of delight, and Maggie singing "Jingle Bells" at the top of her voice. I drag myself from bed and head for the window overlooking the play yard. The shadows paint a surreal scene, in the light dusting of snow and the yellow haze of the street light. Maggie, bare bottomed, dressed in a sleeveless nightgown, is swinging as high as the swing will reach. In the faint light, her long disheveled blond hair fans and sweeps like the tail of a comet. Her tiny bare feet fashion a pointed arc in the night sky. Up the ladder to the slide climbs a brother. A sister gleefully careens to the ground, landing with a plop. Up in an instant, she runs at full speed to take another turn. Two slightly older children giggle in delight as they bump up and down on the seesaw. All are barefoot, clad in worn thin pajamas or night shirts. Joyfully oblivious to the cold, they play in careless abandon.

179

  I stand transfixed; I can't believe my eyes. I look at the roof of the house next door expecting to see Santa in his sleigh. The reindeer prancing and pawing, their breath spreading clouds in the winter night. The elves having abandoned their task, joining the wood nymphs and fairies in play. An ordinary back yard in Chesnee has been recast in storybook beauty.

  The chill of the night brings me back to reality. Oh my! The children will catch their death of cold. I grab a blanket and rush to the door. Jingle bells, jingle bells, jingle all the way, Maggie's voice tinkling like a bell. I slowly lay aside the blanket. There is no place for an adult in this scene. Soon enough their mother will awaken and out will come the switches. I make a mental note to find the Vick's salve, a kettle, and a box of Kleenex, to tuck in with the Christmas candy. Taking the warmth of the children's happiness with me, back to my bed I go. My voice joins with Maggie's as we sing, jingle bells, jingle bells, jingle all the way.

Christmas at Camp Wadsworth
1917

"The weather prevented a pageant; the roads were slushy
with half-melted snow, and it was bitter cold. Lighted Christmas
trees and carols and concerts cheered town and camp. Northerners
were shocked by the typically Southern celebration of Christmas
with fireworks, and Spartans were shocked to learn that such a
mode of celebration was not universal."

*—From "A History of Spartanburg County," compiled by the
Spartanburg Unit of the Writers' Program of the
Works Projects Administration (1940).*

26

A Hometown Christmas
By Lisa Wells Isenhower

I stumbled around our cluttered attic on a cold afternoon last December, looking for the box that held our Christmas lights. I knew the box was there somewhere, clearly labeled and ready to use, but during the eleven months since I'd last had it out, other boxes of treasures and bags of cast-offs had covered it. I spotted the box, finally, under a box of old Revere Ware pans. A box of Christmas lights, three strings of white lights, four strings of colored ones, the little miniature kind.

183

I remembered the year we bought our first Christmas lights, just two strings of white miniatures from Rose's Discount Store on Spartanburg's west side. It was our first Christmas together and our son Rob's first Christmas, and I was determined to put up a tree, though we had no lights, no stand, no decorations, and no plans to actually be in Spartanburg for Christmas. We bought a little six-

foot balsam tree from the Optimists on Reidville
Road and spent a frustrating hour and a half ma-
neuvering it into a wobbly, three-legged stand.
Other than the sparse white lights, our only decorations were red-and-green plaid ribbons and some
tiny candy canes, also purchased at Rose's for a few
dollars. It wasn't quite as bad as Charlie Brown's
tree, but it wasn't exactly a beauty either. Yet it
was important: I had to have a tree that year. I had
to try to make our little house in Park Hills feel like
a home.

When I was growing up as the daughter of a
military officer, having a place to call home had been
very important to me. My family moved every few
years during my childhood, and so I never had a
hometown. Home was just the house we lived in
at the time, not a town one could return to after
years of prodigality, not a community where family
names and place names were woven together inex-
tricably. When I met my husband Bob and visited
his little hometown in North Carolina, I was
charmed by the easy intimacy of the people there.
Everyone knew Bob; he couldn't walk down the
street without meeting someone who knew him,
had known him as a child, had probably known his
parents when they were children. I was envious of
his hometown experience, and realized with regret
that it was something I'd never have. Though I
didn't think of it that way at the time, putting up a
Christmas tree that first year was my way of laying

claim to a hometown of sorts, an attempt to create the kind of history for us that would let us call Spartanburg home.

Over the years, our Christmas trees grew more expensive, our decorations more elaborate, more eclectic. We added more lights; we collected ornaments; we abandoned the ribbons in favor of glass balls. The year our second son, Andrew, was a toddler, we had to remove the candy canes after we discovered that Andrew had tasted a number of them and then tucked them in unexpected places, like the inside of Bob's shoe. As our boys grew and went to school, decorations made of construction paper, glitter, and pipecleaners, clumsily autographed in childish printing on the back, joined our collection of ornaments. Paper-plate doves (with brads to secure their paper-plate wings), clothespin soldiers, macaroni angels, and handprint reindeer became part of our treasure, carefully nestled in tissue paper and saved from year to year. As the boys grew older, the understated white lights gave way to brightly colored ones, and a light-up star that bordered on tacky was installed on the treetop at Andrew's insistence.

185

As our family grew, so did Spartanburg. We moved from our little place in Park Hills to a larger home on the west side of town. Shopping centers and subdivisions sprang up around us. The Optimists no longer ran a tree stand on Reidville Road; they moved to a location near Westgate Mall.

Some years we bought our Christmas tree from the produce stand on Blackstock Road in Arcadia, or from the YMCA sale on Pine Street near our church. For several years we drove north, to Avery County, North Carolina, to choose and cut our own Frasier fir. The boys loved those trips, scrambling over the frosty hillside, discovering a new favorite tree over every rise: "*This* one, Mom! No, wait, I like *this* one! What about *this* one?"

Last year, after Bob suffered a mild stroke before Thanksgiving, our tree buying came full circle. Unable to make the trip to Avery County, we ended up back at the Optimists' stand, near our bank on Ezell Boulevard. We had stopped at the bank after picking Andrew up from school one Friday afternoon. Andrew spotted the trees right away and asked if he could look. "Sure, go ahead," Bob answered. I smiled at Andrew as he strode purposefully toward the trees, and I thought of the little Balsam we had purchased fifteen years before.

Andrew chose a beauty that day, a fragrant Frasier fir that was full and tall. We bundled it into the trunk of Bob's old Peugeot and drove home to put it up. As I scoured the attic for the box of lights, the four boxes of ornaments, and the sturdy, cast-iron stand that had long since replaced our first wobbly tripod, I had to smile. I knew that the home I had been searching for, and never expecting to find, had grown up around me over the past fifteen years. I realized with a start of surprise that the years I had spent in Spartanburg would soon out-number the years I spent moving from place to place.

Now when I walk down the corridors of Westgate Mall, or browse in the library's Westside Branch, or help the Goodfellows pack groceries at the National Guard Armory, I meet people who know me, people who have watched my children grow up, people with whom I have the easy intimacy of long acquaintance. This Christmas, I will probably not be able to find that box of Christmas lights right away. It will be lurking under one of many stacks of stuff in an attic that Bob and I will vow (again) to clean out when the weather warms up. I will probably want to drive to Avery County to cut a Christmas tree, but I'll be content to visit the Optimists' stand instead. I'll no doubt complain about the traffic on the west side of town, and swear I'm never going shopping the day after Thanksgiving again. And one more thing: I'll spend this Christmas in my hometown. In Spartanburg.

187

27

ITALIAN FOR CHRISTMAS
By Marc Henderson

My grandfather Jerry Antonelli, whom all the grandchildren called "Papa Jerry," was second-generation Italian-American. He bore a six-foot frame, heavy with years of manual labor and eating well. His skin was permanently tanned olive and his snowy-white hair was combed straight back in the traditional Italian style. When he laughed, it started deep within and burst out of his massive body. Papa Jerry was my mother's father, my grandfather.

Old black-and-white photos of him and his brothers, when they were young in New York City, show them smiling, well-dressed, arm-in-arm, seated around a large table full of food and wine. Years after these photographs were taken, my grandfather cooked similar meals for our family, especially on Christmas Eve.

When I was a child, Christmas began with a two-day car trip with my family from our home in

Kansas City to my grandparents' houses in
Spartanburg. My parents grew up, met, and married in Spartanburg. But my father's work took
them from the South and eventually out west to
Kansas City and then to Boulder. My first memories of life were of a cold, snowy Kansas City winter.

Our refuge from the cold weather was a
week's stay for Christmas in Spartanburg. And that
meant Christmas Eve at my Grandmother and
Grandfather Antonelli's house.

Papa Jerry started cooking Christmas Eve
dinner early in the morning, or often, the night
before. By noon the house would be filled with the
smells of spicy sauces, yeasty breads, baked sweets,
and the sounds of Italian operas. As Papa Jerry
cooked I would sometimes play behind my grandparents' house in the woods that ended at Lawson's
Fork. When I walked through the kitchen to go
outside, Papa Jerry would stop me. "Maaarc, taste
this sauce," he'd say. "Too much garlic? Try dis
too. Da breads just finished. Take zoome whit you
on the way out. It'd cold out dare." His accent was
as New York as it was Italian.

Papa Jerry came to Spartanburg to train at
Camp Croft during World War II. He and my grandmother, Edith Cash from Chesnee, met while she
was working at the USO. On their first date, they
went to a movie at the Palmetto theater on Main
Street. When the war ended, Papa Jerry, a New

York Catholic, came back to Spartanburg and married his quiet, farm fresh, Southern Baptist sweetheart. Love is never easy.

By the time I'd come back from my walks in the woods, the house would be filling with other family members. My other grandmother, Lois Henderson, would be chasing my young sister through the living room for an armful of grandmotherly love.

"Heather, give me some sugar," she'd say, in her southern way of referring to a kiss. My other grandfather, J.C. Henderson, would be in the kitchen making easy conversation with Papa Jerry. They were good friends.

"Dinner's ready," Papa Jerry would bellow from over the steamy pots on the stove.

Soon, we'd all be seated around the dining room table with platters of Papa Jerry's labor being passed among the diners. The smells of the herbs and spices in the food made it hard to contain our appetites any longer. This was not lofty cuisine, burdened with the unnecessary. It was food of the simple Italian family, just like my Papa Jerry's family was, and our family is today. It was food eaten to live and work on. The pastas were big noodles. The meatballs were as big as golf balls and made the best spicy sandwiches the next day. Around the table, there were bowls of golden green olive oil with raw garlic and melted butter for dipping the bread. The garlic at these Christmas dinners would light up your nose like a red-nosed reindeer, and the bread melted away in your mouth.

At least two bottles of red wine were opened and passed around. And like a family communion, the children were allowed small amounts. No glass remained empty for long.

This one family sounded like an entire restaurant, with its clanging silverware, plates, glasses, and conversations. Papa Jerry, at the head of the table, smiled wide and warm as we enjoyed our dinner. This meal was a gift of himself given to us all on Christmas Eve. When he saw somebody's plate getting light with food, he would have it passed back down the table for a refill.

"Gary—pass me your plate, dare. You need mo," Papa Jerry would say.

"No, really, I'm really full," my dad would protest.

"E-dit," he'd say to my grandmother in his Bronx accent, with a touch of what living in the South for more than thirty years added to the way he spoke. "Pass me Gary's plate, would ya?"

Dinner often ended two hours or more after grace was said, and always with plenty of sweet cakes, custard pies, and coffee. Papa Jerry drank espresso coffee with heavy sugar and finished it all off with the smoke of unfiltered Camels.

Later that night, after midnight church service and when the house was cold and pleasantly dark, I would wrap myself in old blankets from the cedar closet, and have a long Christmas hibernation.

Early Christmas morning, Papa Jerry's heavy limping gate would wake me as he walked across the floor above. It might just as well have been Santa Claus, with his bag of toys slung heavy over his shoulder. I would go on upstairs where my grandmother would now be up and sitting with him at the breakfast counter. She would be eating Raisin Bran and he'd be drinking coffee. A lit Camel would hang from his lip and across his lap would be an old guitar.

"Marco! Help yourself to da coffee," he'd say, never asking if my parents allowed me to drink coffee at my age. "What you want for your breakfast, ayy? Cake? Have some cake then! . . . nobody will know . . ."

The three of us would sit at the counter waiting for everybody else to get up and give Christmas a second wind. Papa Jerry would play the old, poorly tuned guitar and sing Italian love songs to my grandmother, while I ate forbidden cake, trying my best to like coffee the way he did. And my grandmother ate Raisin Bran with her hand over her mouth, laughing and blushing at Papa Jerry's crooning. This unworldly farm girl from Chesnee knew more Italian than we thought she did.

It's been ten years since the last of these Christmas Eve feasts. Papa Jerry died seven years ago and my grandmother Antonelli died in the summer of 1996, just a few months after my other grandmother died in the early days of spring.

Six years ago my family and I moved back to Spartanburg, so my mom and dad could help care for their ailing parents. When my grandmother Antonelli died, they moved into her house. Last Christmas, our family started a new tradition. The house was full of people once again.

The family is smaller, the table less crowded, and the house is not as loud since the grandchildren have grown up. My grandfather Henderson—I now call him J.C.—was there, seeming to be either the newest king or the very last man of his generation. On Christmas Eve afternoon everyone went out for last-minute shopping, leaving me home alone. I sat at the kitchen counter, eating cold lasagna right out of the pan that I'd found in the refrigerator. I drank red wine from a glass tumbler and played one of my Papa Jerry's scratchy old opera albums. The singer's voice was deep, rich, Italian, and miserable with grief. Just for a moment, I smelled the smoke from unfiltered Camels, heard the laughter, and felt the warmth one last time.

Christmas in Downtown Spartanburg
1946

195

"It was Monday, Nov. 25, 1946, at 3 p.m. that the curtains went up and Buck presented his first 'Night Before Christmas' in the very wide and sweeping windows of the Aug. W. Smith Co. ...

The papier mâché figures were about one-third life size and encompassed the whole storefront. As someone said, 'a wonderment,' the first of its kind ever seen in these parts."

*—Reflections on James "Buck" Buchanan's first diorama in
downtown Spartanburg, recorded by Frank Coleman
in "The Daniel Morgan Register."*

28

MEMORIES AT THE WURLITZER
By C. Mack Amick

I t was Christmas 1979, and my Aunt Nanna Mae's small house on Briarwood Road was about as festive as any house could be that Christmas night. The house looked like the top of an old person's birthday cake when the candles are lit. At least that's the way I remember it. I think it was probably after the second or third mug of Aunt Mae's eggnog that things got even more festive. Oh, it was a Christmas to remember all right. For me, many details of Christmases past seem to run together. But Christmas 1979 is one I will never forget.

I was in the Navy and stationed in New England, home for the holidays. So many people to see, so little time, or so it seemed. I guess it was really that way every time I was home. But the rush to see family and friends at Christmas was even more pressing. After all, that's *the* time to do those things. However, my family and I knew that in spite of the holiday chaos, going to Aunt Mae's would be the one constant, the one place we would not miss visiting.

Aunt Mae's was a special place. Not only did I learn to drink scotch at Aunt Mae's (when I was in college, of course), but it was also the first place I ever remember seeing more than one fork at every plate. More than one glass, too. And always a candle on the table. What's more, we *lit* the candles when we ate at Mae's! We just didn't do those things at home. And there was always a snack available for a young visitor—all those things you couldn't get anywhere else. Yep, she was special all right. Took a real interest in us kids. A real listener. Some are real talkers. Mae, she was a real listener. I cannot remember a single quote or witticism attributable to her, but I can see her sitting and listening intently to any story a child might tell. She always seemed to have the time for any niece or nephew who visited. And we returned the favor. We loved her and loved being around her.

So it was easy to be in the holiday spirit when at Aunt Mae's. The scene being played out at her house that particular night was most assuredly being played out all over Spartanburg. But for me, it was the center of the universe! A universe where my mom, my aunt, my brothers, and I and all of our families wanted to be that Christmas.

It didn't take long to settle in once there. The nog helped and it was the good stuff. It was

198

during this time, when the final touches to the meal were being put in place, that conversation grew more lively, the kids got louder and that we all, consciously or not, soaked up every moment of what was happening.

The tradition was to eat late at Mae's. So eventually a huge lasagna dinner was served. Okay, so maybe *that* particular menu wasn't typical fare for Christmas in Spartanburg. But it was just another one of those things that made being at Mae's so special and so different—so "cosmopolitan," as I would later learn to appreciate.

After dinner, there was the cleanup, dessert, maybe some TV. Gifts weren't normally exchanged at Aunt Mae's. That had already happened at our respective homes that morning. It was what would come later that made these types of gatherings at Mae's so special. Aunt Mae would make a move toward the Wurlitzer, clear the organ bench of magazines and the telephone, and finally pull out the bench and sit down. There was no particular signal for this to be done. Mae seemed to know when it was time. She led. We followed. Some of us gathered around the organ, some of us sat round the small den—some on chairs and the couch, some on the floor. This was the high point of the evening all right. And we knew it.

199

The sheet music and hymn books were given out. Mae would do a few bars of one Christmas carol, then move on to another. This was her warm up, she would say. This ritual also served to get everyone in the spirit. And everyone did eventually get in the spirit; even my more reserved middle brother—the kids, my mom, my youngest brother—everyone. The singing went on for a while, until every last carol—some known, some unknown—had been played and sung. But kids get tired, the hours pass, and long drives home have to be made, even if it is Christmas.

So there was a point at which everyone began to gather up kids, doggy bags, and coats. Another Christmas tucked away to fondly recall. But my youngest brother, Cliff, made it clear that he was not ready to go home—not yet anyway. Oh, he wasn't loud about it, but firmly asked me to stay and sing more Christmas carols. I had had just enough of Mae's nog that I was still in the spirit, so to speak. So my arm didn't have to be twisted. And Mae was ready to go another round or two, of playing the organ, that is. Even Mom decided to stay and give us moral support. So all the wives, kids, and my middle brother, Robert, made their way home, and we stayed a while longer.

At twenty-seven, Cliff was the youngest brother; six years my junior. He was more like me than any other brother. Animated. Outwardly sensitive. Thought nothing of giving me a big bear hug when I would come home. Also thought nothing of breaking into a song at a moment's notice. I think he always thought he should be on stage somewhere. And he was truly in the spirit that night!

Mind you, it was approaching midnight and there we were, Cliff, Aunt Mae, my mom, and I, singing and playing at the top of our lungs, one carol after another; some in key, some not. I think at one point, we even walked out on the porch and serenaded all of Briarwood Road. I suppose this went on for an hour or so and then we, too, reached our limit. The caroling session to end all caroling sessions was over. The good-byes seemed extra long that night. But Cliff seemed to want to linger now as I think about it.

That was Cliff's last Christmas—on this earth, anyway. Funny, seems like he knew it, crazy as that sounds. On election day, the next year, he was killed by a drunken driver in an auto accident. I guess that's why the Christmas of '79, on Spartanburg's Briarwood Road, will always be one of the most memorable for me. Needless to say, similar gatherings at Mae's after that Christmas just weren't the same. Now, every time I am in Aunt Mae's house, I pause for a moment as I walk past the Wurlitzer, and remember that Christmas night many years ago.

THE CHRISTMAS SAW

By Gene Lassiter

When I came to South Carolina twenty-four years ago, I found it hard to understand the locals. It is so easy to classify the people one does not know well as backward. I learned an early lesson about just such a thing while pastoring a small church not too far from the Spartanburg city limits.

203

"Preacher, we want you to come to our community Christmas supper. We always have it in the old post office."

"There's an old post office here?"

"Sure there is, and Sam is going to provide the music."

"Sam!" The thought of Sam making music of any kind was a bit startling. I had known Sam for over a year, preached to him every Sunday afternoon, and had actually been inside his house, once.

Sam always ambled up the old wooden steps

of the Presbyterian Church promptly at 2:50 p.m., pulled open the double screen doors and strode down the aisle, taking his regular seat in the front pew, left side, three places in from one of the hand-carved end posts. Depending on how long it had been since Sam had sent his suit to the cleaners, he might have the entire left side of the church to himself. If the breeze was just right, the fumes of years of bat guano and Sam's pack of twenty or so breed-challenged canines would sweep up to the pulpit just as Sam sat down. About the same time, the cloud of sulfurous scent would settle on the assembled brothers and sisters sitting behind Sam, and there would be a choked exodus to the far wall on the right. Sam, of course, gave no notice to our discomfort and sat straight as a ramrod, waiting for the Word of the Lord to be bestowed upon his faithful heart. The suit in question was the same one bought by his mother when Sam had returned from the Great War of trenches and Black Jack Pershing, of Sopwith Camels and the Red Baron. Sam had been one of Black Jack's "Doughboys." In fact he still had his uniform hanging on a rack in the living room of the house he occupied with the bats and dogs.

I had gone to visit Sam on a hot July day and regretted the decision twenty yards from the front porch. Sitting in the swing, he motioned for me to come up and join him. Step by step, I plunged deeper into a cloud of acrid, sickly sweet fumes that

204

surrounded the old house. It stuck in my throat
and I almost turned and fled to clear air. Sam rose
with an angelic smile on his face, welcomed me to
his home and offered a seat in the worn, ladder-
back oak chair that seems to haunt every porch in
rural South Carolina. "Not many come to visit me,"
he said. And he began to laugh with what can only
be described as a cross between a rusty gate swinging in a gale, and a three-pack-a-day cancerous
cough. He must have noticed the green pallor on
my face and the looming tears at the corners of my
eyes. "You get used to the smell after a while."
There followed more cackling and snorting.

A trip inside the old house revealed a foot-
long double-blade knife switch that turned on a
single, seventy-five-watt bulb hanging on a six-foot
twisted cord from high planked ceilings. There
were two rooms on the first floor, one to each side
of a central hall that ran from front door to back
door. As we entered the front door, several of the
dogs raced in with us and ran up the stairs to the
second floor. With yells and scoldings, Sam was able
to coax them back outside.

205

"They sleep up there, with the bats." More
cackling and snarfing.

The truth was I really was getting used to
the smell. The choking had stopped and there remained only a slight feeling as if something were
hanging about the end of my nose; a net-like sen-
sation of sickly sweet, rotting manure wafting about

my head. Sam opened the door on the left and took me into a room that surely had not been disturbed in years. There was an old square piano in the middle of the room, with what appeared to be a flower-print covered sofa on one side and a wooden arm chair to the other. Hanging on a clothes rack, as if at attention, was the Doughboy uniform, ready to march off should "Black Jack" ever call again. We returned to the central hall and Sam proudly pointed out the shelves of books climbing to the ceiling. He pulled down a volume of Shakespeare printed in "Charlestown" in the 1760s, and without opening the pages began to quote from "Julius Caesar." In that raspy old voice he went on and on until I broke in, amazed, and said, "Sam, just how much of that play have you memorized?"

"All of it. I used to be able to say the entire thing. Along with 'King Lear' and 'Macbeth,' and 'Hamlet,' but old age has got to me. I learned to read with this library, right in this house. Mama sat me down each night and read to me and made me read back to her."

A week before Christmas, I arrived at the little clapboard building prepared to witness Sam's humiliation. Why, I had heard Sam sing Sunday after Sunday and he could not carry a tune in that proverbial bucket. This was going to be a real hoot, a laugher if ever there was one. There was food aplenty and the kind of warm fellowship that can only be enjoyed in a small rural community where everybody knows everything about everybody and still loves them. After a few presents had been given to the folks who saw to the arrangements, Sam was called forward. The suit had been to the cleaners the week previous so no one ran for the doors. In fact there was a general sense of expectancy and excitement that puzzled me. These folks are actually looking forward to this, I thought.

It was then that I noticed Sam reaching behind the wood stove to bring out something wrapped in a sheet. When he carefully folded back the yellowed cloth, there was a shiny saw, a common handsaw and a violin bow. Sam took a seat and placed the handle of the saw between his legs and clasped the metal end in his left hand, bending the saw into a crescent that reflected the flames in the old stove. Sam drew the bow over the back edge of the saw and wonder settled over the old post office. "O Come All Ye Faithful" filled the room in such clear notes that none of us seemed to be breathing for a moment. Carol after carol soared from the saw until "Silent Night" brought from our throats the murmurs of " . . . sleep in heavenly peace, sleep in heavenly peace." There was such a look of joy on that wrinkled old face as he carefully wrapped the bow and the saw until next year.

207

Then One Zoggy Christmas
By Sam Howie

On Christmas Eve 1996, I heard my mother say about my then four-year-old niece, "This will be *the* Christmas for her. This will be *the* one."

I knew exactly what she meant. Three days before, on my traditional solstice excursion to Westgate Mall (where the winter dearth of natural light was nicely balanced by the surplus of Christmas bulbs) I had seen the blessed anticipation of *the* Christmas displayed prominently and unmistakably across the faces of Spartanburg's children. You could almost see in their countenances the dancing visions of sugar-plums. Well, perhaps they were visions of Nintendo 64s, or visions of Tickle Me Elmo dolls, but there were definitely *visions* going on in the minds of our city's young citizens, visions of a Christmas greater than the one I was feeling at the moment. Yet somehow I empathized with them, those beaming little guardians of the magical yuletide secrets. I knew their job, if only tangentially. I was distantly privy to their sacred Christmas secrets because I too had once been gripped by the dazzling charm of *the* Christmas.

It was not hard at all for me to recall the Christmas which had served as *the* Christmas for me, though only upon careful reflection have I construed what *the* Christmas really means. *The* Christmas, I have come to define, is the one when Christmas magic, elusive and distorted in subsequent years, is at its resplendent and unadulterated best. It is the one when you are just old enough to develop a wonderfully simplistic understanding of Santa Claus, believing him to be concrete, so that those *Yes, Virginia . . . He's the Spirit of Giving* type abstractions are unnecessary.

For me, *the* Christmas was the one when my sister made waxy-tasting cookies in her new Easy Bake Oven, and I got a Kennedy half dollar in the toe of my stocking, though these events were incidental. *The* Christmas, above all else, was the Christmas of Zog.

Zog was a robot suit, an unsolicited present I found waiting on me Christmas morning. At first I thought it was inferior to my neighbor's New York Jets uniform, but I quickly discovered that donning the Zog apparel transcended mere dress-up. It was something akin to metempsychosis, so that I became Zog, and furthermore, Zog became whomever I wanted him to be.

His character formed quickly. Zog was strong as Popeye, but candy canes were his spinach. Zog's IQ was off the scale, and he was exceedingly personable. Zog was in charge, and I was young enough to believe that those in charge were sufficiently steeped in both competence and integrity. My pretensions made Zog righteously powerful. Zog protected the universe from evil, using only a stick from a pecan tree as a laser gun. Zog rescued imaginary damsels. Zog frightened away an evil little yappy Chihuahua who happened by the yard, but befriended my own German shepherd.

Zog was Great. Zog was Good. Zog was, essentially, a cheap collection of gray-colored cardboard.

He had some simple geometric figures, inked in red and orange and yellow, which represented his mechanical orifices. Some jagged yellow designs across his abdomen, his electronic guts, supposedly the ultimate of 1960s technology, resembled nothing so much as an ocular migraine headache. His entire mass, including the ink that colored him, was not worth more than one or two 1967 dollars, but then, neither is the human being valuable when appraised according to physical elements. As in the case with most worthwhile human enterprise, Zog's value was the result of imagination in union with goodness.

Christmas for me since then has been what I imagine to be a pretty typical, perhaps universal

211

experience. I have seen the waning of that early Christmas magic, and, consequently, the dark forces of the anti-Zog have made their presence sharply felt. As disillusionment generally snowballs once it begins, I have been blitzed by the tragic adult realization that those in charge of running the world, the unZogged Powers That Be, often lack competence, integrity, or both. The yappie little Chihuahuas, which Zog zapped like so many gnats in a purple bug-zapped light, too often become powerful politicians, business leaders, and bureaucrats. The waning of Christmas magic, for me, coincided with the brutal adult recognition of the general ineptitude of civilization. Recognizing this link, I have always sought to rekindle that early Christmas magic in hopes that it would also rekindle my faith in civilization.

For a time, as my penchant for materialism and consumer sophistication robotically obeyed the little of DNA which codes us to be Americans (worshippers of The Product, collectors of consecrated Stuff), I made the typical American mistake of believing that the price of the Christmas present is the fact that determines the extent to which Christmas is magic. My level of satisfaction at Christmas came to be directly proportionate to the number of dollars spent on the presents I received. But not even the expensive Les Paul guitar I received as a teenager was enough to emulate the power of Zog, and I did not know whether to be happy or sad upon realizing that no amount of money could buy Christmas magic.

Among the wasteland of expensive widgets, wadgets, and whatchamacallits in my Christmas memories, there are some odd but poignant images. Zog is the most notable of these, but there are many more. One that comes to mind is of a poor kid my mom taught in her second-grade class. On the day that the class wrote letters to Santa Claus, according to my mom, most of the kids were compiling long lists of requests for bikes and dolls and video games and remote control cars and candy and more toys and more candy and lots and lots and lots of surprises. This one kid asked only for a box of crayons. This was a kid, I believe, who would have truly appreciated a Zog suit. Though I never met him, I think of him every Christmas.

My image of that kid is woven into the nebula of sad and sacred Christmas images that work to give me an ever-evolving, sketchy outline of the Christmas ideal. The outline seems to simultaneously dull and sharpen with each new Christmas memory. Perhaps I will never fully understand the mystery of a season when magic so sweetly surfeits some while bitterly eluding others, but of this much I feel confident. The value of Christmas, greater than the sum of its parts and more confusing and bittersweet with each passing year, is more accessible to those who have sanctified some core Christmas image, be it savior, Saint

213

Nick, or something so unlikely as a box of crayons or a cardboard robot suit. Around this core of sacrosanct certainty, the more ambiguous matter of the Christmas experience may be hazily spun.

From this revelation, a greater understanding of *the* Christmas seems to have flowed quite naturally for me. *The* Christmas, the one when the magic is sharp and pure, the same one you will surely see on a hundred tiny faces if you venture to Pine Street for the annual Christmas parade, is the core of my ongoing Christmas experience. And so it follows that remembering that long-ago Christmas accomplishes more than the mere servicing of nostalgia and wishfulness. *The* Christmas lives immutably, coloring the joys and assuaging the pains of all the other Christmases. "Some good, sacred Christmas memory," to put a seasonal spin on Dostoyevsky, "is perhaps the best education." For me, that sacred yuletide experience was . . . is the Christmas of Zog.

214

**Christmas in Downtown Spartanburg
1950s**

215

"They used to virtually put the entire Morgan Square under
a canopy of living garlands and multicolored lights . . . It was
a big deal to go into town and see the decorations. The canopy
over the square—when you drove under that, it was gorgeous.
It really was."

—*Buddy Womick, quoted in the Spartanburg Herald-
Journal (1989).*

AFTER THE ROBINS CAME
By Robin Ely Carroll

Saturday morning, the house is quiet, and I am alone. The children are playing basketball at church, and Michael is dutifully watching them prove their athletic prowess. I must admit I am melancholy. Christmas is over, the decorations are tucked away in the attic for another year, and I am not looking forward to a gray January. I stand at my kitchen window, drinking my warm coffee, and contemplate the grayness of the sky. I stand at the window, a creature of habit.

217

From the window, I see the old canning house that we turned into a playhouse for the children last summer. The children helped me paint the walls the color of the summer sky (a true Carolina blue). We laid a new linoleum tile floor and placed "real" bookshelves, end tables, and a love seat against the walls and put shutters on the windows to make it look like a miniature home. I question

myself how the children could have already out-
grown it (they asked me recently if I would turn it
into "the little library house" and have Daddy run
electricity to it), and I realize it was two summers
ago that we had the "renovation;" not last year, and
like everything else of late, time has slipped up on
me again on this one, too.

The kitchen window is one of my favorite
places from which to view the outside world. I look
out upon the soon-to-be "little library house," the
towering pecan and cedar trees, my two St. Francis
statues with their continual offerings of sunflower
seeds and millet and occasional bread crumbs, and
the old tin-roofed barn currently serving as a large
doghouse for our four dogs. I admire the beauty of
the back pasture as it rolls into the woods at the
edge of the ravine—the ravine which, when swol-
len with rain, creates a watery path past the dairy
farm to the old Anderson Mill on the banks of the
Tyger River. And I admire the grooming work of
my husband for making the pasture look more beautiful than any golf course fairway anywhere. I am
happy here.

I watch the mourning doves slowly and me-
thodically wobble around the old wellhead to nibble
at the crumbs scattered by the sparrows. The car-
dinals come too, but they eat, do not make a mess,
and do not walk in their food. They are beautiful
creatures, especially the boys, and they behave as
if they know it. I watch as the mockingbirds choose

their fence posts, establish their territory, and swoop down through the cedars to chase off a worm-eating bird from the yard of the "little library house." I think of my friend Susan who told me once that you have everything in the world to be thankful for if you have a bird outside your window.

I watch as one of the mockingbirds pursues a robin over the fence into the back pasture. Was that a robin? It's not springtime, I think. Surely not. I chuckle at the memory of my brothers and me setting shoeboxes in the back yard, propped up by sticks, and running with Morton salt boxes in our hands, " . . . if you get close enough to the robins to put salt on their tails, you can catch them." Robins—springtime, the first sighting, who saw the first one? Running around the yard with my brothers trying to catch the worm-eaters who never eat the seeds set out by the humans. And then I realize the back pasture is covered with birds. But these aren't just birds, they are robins. I wanted to count them as I knew no one would believe me. There were eighty, ninety, over one hundred in our yard. They were covering the field. Where are the dogs?

My mind is swirling in the loveliness of the memories of robins—springtime, the sighting of the first robin. My mind swirls around the numbers. . . eighty, ninety, one hundred; and I realize I am playing out the accountant mentality side of me rather than enjoying the true beauty of it all. The dogs do not come. The robins eat, they nourish themselves,

219

and they stay for a while. There is no one or nothing to startle them away. They know the territory of the mockingbirds who stay on the fence posts in the cedars, and the robins respect those boundaries.

I feel the memory of my childhood springtime, and realize that too often we take for granted the geography of our childhood. Engrained in our very being long after we leave the environs of our youth are the tucked-away memories of the sweet, simple pleasures of the days when the world around us was full of laughter, color, fragrance, and love. Our very being and existence as adults is shaped by where we were or where we were not and what we did or did not do when we were little people. My memory spirals forward from running through the yard with my Morton salt box to my three Royal Copenhagen robins in my curio cabinet . . . the mama and the two baby birds. As with all that happens to me and all that I witness in life, I search for a meaning, a pattern, a link to my life. Why did the robins come now and so many of them? It was almost surreal—like a Salvador Dali painting, but sweet, not foreboding—a true epiphany.

It's the Christmas season, not springtime.

That night, as the ice pelted against our windows, I thought of the robins. They had not the privilege of listening to weather reports, but they knew the storm was coming. They ate from a field bountiful in the food that nourished them. They ate, and they traveled on before the storm came.

How did they know?

On Sunday, we awakened to a bright, white glistening world. My melancholy had passed with the changing of the barometric pressure, the visit from the robins, and the blanketing of snow. The peace of the farm, the snow shovel that stayed in the shed, the bright orange sled, the ice-packed sled train down the side pasture, the drying boots and gloves by the front door, the bright red boy-cardinals at the bird feeder, the blue jays swooping through the cedars, the smell of homemade soup and hot chocolate, the children's laughter, the pink cheeks, the warmth of our home, and the love of my husband and children. We had an abundance of sweet, simple pleasures, and our world was filled with laughter, color, fragrance, and love.

The week passed quickly—too much so, as does all that's good in life. The snow stayed and a new blanket of white was added later in the week. We were warm and we nourished ourselves with the food that feeds our souls.

The robins did not return during the week, nor the week following, but they will be here soon, as springtime is near.

221

32

THE GIFT OF GRIEF
By Deno Trakas

This Christmas was to be the fiftieth wedding anniversary of my parents (they were married in the Greek church in Spartanburg in 1946), and we had planned to have a big party at their home in St. Petersburg, Florida. But my father died suddenly, ungently, in September, so this Christmas became, instead, the first without Dad.

It was a strange, moody time for me. I took a lot of walks in Maximo Moorings, the neighborhood where I grew up, which was an easy bike ride from the college where my father taught and a comfortable place to learn tennis, basketball, baseball, and the box step at our teen cotillion. During Christmas week the temperature rose to the low eighties every afternoon, which cast a surreal shimmer over our stay, although I remember it being just as muggy at Christmas when I got my first skateboard. On one of my walks I saw a scene that summed up my conflicted feelings. One flat Florida house was decorated with a tacky tableau of lights on strings wrapped around cactus and hibiscus as a backdrop for a glowing plastic four-foot-high nativity scene. The house next door was adorned with a single large but understated wreath of evergreens tied with a red velvet ribbon—and inside the wreath was a small wooden cross. And next door to that was a house with no decorations except a banner on a flag pole which read "BAH HUMBUG!" That's how I felt: contemptuous of the gaudy displays of the season; appreciative of the subtle power of a cross to evoke the awesome story of Christ's birth, which was as much religion as my short-winded spirit could handle; but also downright grumpy and Scroogey.

224

I'm sure the mood had to do with the loss of my father, but his absence was less tangible than I'd expected. His role at Christmas had diminished over the years as we children grew up and had children of our own. On Christmas morning, he usually sat in a straightback chair that he carried in from the dining room; from there he observed, forgetful of what he had given and embarrassed by what he received. Of course he delighted in the rapture on the faces of the little ones, but he grew impatient with the prolonged exchange of gifts. He had things to do—trash to take out and breakfast to make, his famous scrambled eggs and biscuits.

This year he wasn't there, our lord and servant. As we piled out of the van after our twelve-hour trip from Spartanburg, he wasn't there, coming through the carport to greet us with hearty hugs and scratchy kisses and a gallon of homemade ice cream hardening in the freezer.

He wasn't there to cut the grass or pick the tangerines off his trees or make frequent runs to the grocery store, which he loved to do. No matter what he went for, a dozen eggs or a pound of feta cheese, he always came back with several full bags, and one always had a pie or box of donuts. Always better to have more than enough than not enough—that was his motto when his kids were visiting, a consequence, I suppose, of being raised during the Depression with nine hungry brothers and sisters.

225

He wasn't there at the piano, practicing for his next recital—he had played the piano by ear since he was a boy, but in his retirement he took lessons from a Suzuki master and proudly performed with the other beginning students, most of whom were six years old.

He wasn't there in his chair at the end of the dining room table, with a floor lamp beside him and his briefcase open in front of him, grading papers deep into the night.

He wasn't there to set up the card table and play Canasta or Oh Hell with Mom and my children until 2:00 or 3:00 a.m., and he wasn't there the next morning, awake by 9:00 and ready to take orders in spite of staying up so late.

He wasn't there to get us up for church, to remind us of those dreaded Sunday mornings when he would be in a foul mood because we were running late and we *were* the choir—Dad the director, Mom the organist, and all five of us kids singers.

He wasn't there to show us, with every aching gesture, with every stooped favor, that he loved us.

I went looking for him. I had an errand to run at the library and planned to go from there to the cemetery. I'd asked Mom the address because although I grew up in St. Petersburg, I'd never paid much attention to its burial grounds, but she misheard me and gave me the address of the library. I didn't realize it until I was at the library, so I looked up "cemetery" in the phone book. There were two. I tried to remember the tear-blurred ride in the hearse from the funeral home in September and headed for the one on the north side of town. Wrong.

I turned around and went to the other one, and sure enough, the entrance looked familiar, so I drove in and followed my memory toward what I quickly realized was an unmarked grave. My sister had designed a headstone with the Greek Key as a border and a quote from "Hamlet"—"Now cracks a noble heart. Good night, sweet prince, /And flights of angels sing thee to thy rest"—but it hadn't arrived. So I plodded through the spongy St. Augus-

226

tine grass in the area where I thought I remembered standing on that oppressive September day. I found three places where the grass had been dug up and replanted, two of them marked by dying poinsettias. I looked up and heard Dad chuckle. So I watered the potted plants, divided my handful of dried flowers into three small bunches and left one in each spot. I asked Dad if that was okay, and he said of course.

My father gave me his sense of humor, among many other things for which I will always be grateful—for example, he taught me how to be a father—but this Christmas he gave me a final valuable gift: grief. Not the denial, guilt, and tearful, wrenching pain of September, but a thoughtful, reflective, appreciative sense of loss. To live is to feel, and I am most alive when I feel deeply, good or bad. My father's death dug me out, scraped my insides, made me hollow, but it left me a clean vessel ready to be filled again. And it didn't take long for the flow to begin in the form of love and support from those around me. I'll never forget the moment I saw my kids for the first time after hearing of my father's death. It was late afternoon, and I met them at McCracken Junior High, where my soccer team practices. They arrived before me, and as I walked out onto the field, Dylan, twelve, and Hayley, fifteen, came to me and hugged me. My son is still demonstrative with his affections, but my daughter, well, she's fifteen. For her to give me a linger-

227

ing, unselfconscious hug, in public . . . it was more surreal than Christmas in sweaty St. Pete, but mainly it was a blessing.

Wallace Stevens said, "Death is the mother of beauty," and so it is. We can't fully appreciate the splendor of life until we see the gaunt face of death up close. We can't be our full vital selves unless we appreciate, and don't take for granted, our dependence on that single pumping muscle that is the symbol of all we feel. Even the best hearts fail—I know that now.

228

The first Christmas without Dad was moody but not bad. My mother, brothers and sisters and I pulled together and did some of the things that Dad used to do. Chris and I picked the tangerines; Steve took Dad's place at the card table; Hansen fixed the carport post; Mom, Joanne, and Irene did more than their share of the cooking and cleaning; Nyko, Leslie, and Kathy took turns shopping—they bought pies—and so on, trying to fill the void that can't be filled at the center of our family.

BIOGRAPHIES

C. Mack Amick, a retired U.S. Navy Nurse Corps Officer, is a licensed counselor who conducts workshops and seminars nationally on a variety of health and wellness issues. Also host of a weekly Public Broadcasting System public affairs program, he is a frequent writer of health-related articles.

A native Spartan now living in Colorado, **Anne Alexander Bain** has a master's degree in architecture and enjoys the creative process of coaxing "something" from "nothing"– be it a building, a painting, short story, or poem. Anne's poetry has been published in the *American Poetry Anthology*; her artwork has been published by Impact Publishers; and she has designed buildings in Colorado and North Carolina.

Meg Barnhouse grew up in North Carolina and Philadelphia and has lived in Spartanburg since 1981. After graduating from Duke University and Princeton Seminary, she worked as chaplain of Converse College for six years, teaching in the Religion and the Theater departments. She is now a Unitarian Universalist minister and has a private pastoral counseling practice overlooking Morgan Square. Meg is the mother of two sons, she plays guitar and African drums, writes novels, has a second-degree black belt in karate and is a commentator for North Carolina Public Radio on a segment called "Radio Free Bubba."

231

Linda Powers Bilanchone is an instructor of communications and director of the Media Center at Wofford College. She and her husband, Vic, are restoring an historic house in Hampton Heights. They have three grown children: Patrick, Jodi, and Jill.

Born in Spartanburg County, **Butler Brewton** has published two volumes of poetry, *Rafters* (1995) and *Indian Summer* (1997). After a twenty-five-year career as an associate professor of English at Montclair State University in New Jersey, he has returned to the Upstate to write poetry and teach English classes part-time at Furman University.

Robin Ely Carroll is a mom, a wife, a chauffeur, a part-time C.P.A. and a native Kentuckian who has fallen in love with South Carolina. (The only time she gets homesick is during the playing of "My Old Kentucky Home" at the Derby or Wildcat basketball games). She, her husband, Michael, her children, Margaret and Matthew, and a menagerie of animals live on a small farm in Moore. They spend their "free time" off the farm participating in Revolutionary War re-enactments.

232

Barbara Mather Cobb, who grew up in the dirt and sand of Philadelphia and the Jersey Shore, has been firmly planted in the red clay of Spartanburg since 1993. She teaches English, writes, and enjoys playing with her human and canine family and friends.

Suellen E. Dean grew up in L.A. (Lower Alabama). The mother of three daughters, she has been writing for small-town newspapers for a long time. But she still knows how to thump a ripe watermelon and shell a good mess of purple hulls for supper. She only dreams of moving away.

Georgie Dickerson found her "magic" when she married Bill Dickerson and they produced a daughter and four sons. The magic of family, learning, reading, teaching, painting, writing, and worshipping enriches her life. Her white house in the country near Pacolet is a symbol of peace and commitment where she and Bill spend their lives together and watch their grandchildren grow.

Elaine Lang Ferguson is an Air Force brat born in England, where her parents rented a cottage on a greyhound farm. She moved to Spartanburg in 1983 to marry Michael. She plays percussion with her friend Laurel and the W.H.O. and is learning Tai Chi and Oriental Dance.

Mike Hembree, a resident of Spartanburg and staff writer for *The Greenville News*, has worked in daily newspaper journalism since 1968. He has won numerous national and state newspaper writing awards and is the co-author of four books on Upstate South Carolina history. A believer in Santa Claus, he wants mountain property for Christmas.

Gary Henderson spent his childhood in Spartanburg, then moved west, where he had a marketing company in Kansas City and wrote stories for a Colorado magazine. He returned in 1992 to write news and feature stories for the Spartanburg *Herald-Journal*. In 1995, he wrote *Nine Days in Union: The Search for Michael and Alex Smith*, which was featured on several national news programs. He is a co-founder of the Hub City Writers Project.

233

Marc Henderson grew up in Kansas City, Missouri, and made frequent trips to Spartanburg to visit his grandparents and other relatives. Until 1992, he lived in Boulder, Colorado, where he raced bicycles, studied emergency medicine and wrote articles for *Colorado Peaks* magazine. Marc, a Charleston County paramedic, writes from his home on the South Carolina coast.

Ann Hicks was born in Hungary and came to the United States as a political refugee in 1957. A graduate of the University of South Carolina, she has made her home in

Spartanburg for the past forty years. She is the wife of Joe Hicks and is the mother of a son, a daughter, a Bassett hound, and a cat.

Sam Howie has worked as a mailman, musician, stock broker, office temp, book reviewer, youth counselor, small business consultant, college professor, funeral services telemarketer, and job coach for welfare recipients. Recovering from an expensive addiction to higher education, he now plays the guitar and is learning the banjo, much to the annoyance of his neighbors in Spartanburg, where he lives alone (but is planning to get a dog, just as soon as he gets over his fear of commitment).

A native of Seattle, **Lisa Wells Isenhower** has lived in Spartanburg since 1979 when she moved here to attend college. She teaches composition and creative writing at Spartanburg Methodist College and has published her own work in such magazines as *Guideposts*, *Christian Living*, and *Living Prayer*. When she's not in the classroom or at the word processor, Lisa spends her time on Spartanburg's westside with her husband, Bob, and their two sons, Rob and Andrew.

234

John Lane is a neo-Druid, poet and writer with deep genetic Spartanburg connections. He has published a book of essays (*Weed Time*), two collections of poems (*As the World Around Us Sleeps* and *Against Information and Other Poems*), and a one-act play (*The Pheasant Cage*). He is a co-founder of the Hub City Writers Project and teaches at Wofford College. He spends his summers in a tower near Cullowhee, North Carolina, and is known in Southern literary circles as "the redneck Yeats."

Gene Lassiter, raised in Winterpock, Virginia, has served as pastor of Second Presbyterian Church in Spartanburg for eleven years. A former Army helicopter pilot with two tours in Vietnam, Gene shares six children and four grandchildren with his wife, Nancy.

Jane Mailloux is a Canadian living with her husband and three teen-aged children in Spartanburg. She was educated at McGill University in Montreal and has taught early childhood through adult levels. She has been writing for decades but has only recently been submitting her work for publication.

Carlin Morrison is a Spartanburg transplant, originally from Burlington, North Carolina. She attended Converse College, received a master's degree in English from Clemson University, then returned to make Spartanburg her home. She writes short fiction when not working on opening The Hub City Bakery in downtown Spartanburg.

Kirk Neely, a native of Spartanburg, is pastor of Morningside Baptist Church. He serves on the boards of the Rotary Club of Spartanburg, the Palmetto Council of Boy Scouts of America, St. Luke's Free Clinic, and the Boys and Girls Clubs of Spartanburg. A member of the National Association for the Preservation and Perpetuation of Storytelling, Kirk and his wife, Clare, have five children: Kirk, Erik, Scott, Kris, and Betsy.

235

Nancy Jenkins Ogle is the creator of the award-winning television series, "Upstate Memories" and the Spartanburg County Oral History Project. Her many volunteer activities reflect a deep affection for the people of the Upstate. She is executive director of The Shepherd's Center of Spartanburg and a member of its creative writing class.

Marsha Poliakoff, an award-winning playwright, studied playwriting at Converse College, and has produced plays at Spotlighters' Theatre in Baltimore, Maryland, Converse, and USC-Spartanburg. She is a native of Baltimore and has a master's degree in English with an emphasis in creative writing from the University of South Carolina. She has taught playwriting at the South Carolina Writers Workshop and the Spartanburg County Art Center. She is a past president of the Spartanburg Branch of the National

League of American Pen Women.

Phil Racine teaches history at Wofford College. He and his wife, Frances, have lived in Spartanburg since 1969. They have two children, Russell and Ali.

Ruth Shanor of Cowpens conformed for forty years: housewifing, volunteering, and raising three exceptional kids. Then, burned out, she fled to Spain for twenty-two years where she worked in a laundry, painted, and wrote stories. She finally moved to Spartanburg to share her aged father's last five years. She is a member of the Spartanburg Artists' Guild and author of two books, *Self-Encounter* and *Rear View Mirror*.

Rosa Shand, a professor of English at Converse College, has published more than twenty stories in literary journals. She received "Special Mention" for the Pushcart Prize and is a four-time winner of the South Carolina Fiction Project. She was raised in Columbia and lived in Uganda for ten years.

Cooper Smith, a native and resident of Cherokee County, spent thirty years in the Spartanburg school system and now serves as a municipal judge in Gaffney. His columns about the complexities that structure society have appeared in several regional publications, including *The Charlotte Observer*. One of his short stories, "Raghorn," has been published by the University of South Carolina Press.

Matthew Teague, a native South Carolinian, was schooled at Wofford College in English and philosophy. He now lives in Oxford, Mississippi, where he is an associate editor of *The Oxford American*, "the Southern Magazine of Good Writing."

Betsy Wakefield Teter is a freelance writer and a co-founder of the Hub City Writers Project. She lives in Converse Heights where she directs the Hub City entertainment empire from her dining room table. She loves Walker Percy, beam reaches, watching AYSO soccer, and having coffee on Morgan Square. She is the author of *Spartanburg A-Plenty*, a collection of columns from her newspaper days at the Spartanburg *Herald-Journal*.

Deno Trakas has lived in the "Hub City" for seventeen years, following his ancestors who settled here at the turn of the century. He teaches English and coaches the women's tennis team at Wofford College during the school year. This summer he tried to rehabilitate from Achilles' surgery and technological incompetence, but usually he spends his summers writing fiction or poetry, and he hopes to publish a chapbook of poems, *Human and Puny*, and a novel, *After Paris*, as soon as he can convince his publisher of their merit and market.

A Spartanburg County native, **Gloria Underwood** was raised in Campobello, and after receiving her undergraduate degree at Furman University, she spent her early adulthood in Spartanburg. After a brief stay in Columbia, where she received her doctorate in contemporary American literature from the University of South Carolina, she moved to Bluffton, South Carolina, and teaches at Savannah College of Art and Design.

237

After graduating from Winthrop College, **Evelyn Brock Waldrop** taught music and English in California and Florida before returning to South Carolina, where she has done agency and freelance copywriting, hosted a daily radio interview show, and was publicity director for a college, a symphony, a social service agency, and textile accounts. Now living in Greenville, she is still writing newsletters, press releases, and trade magazine articles. She promises to retire at age one hundred.

The Hub City Writers Project is a diverse group of local authors whose purpose is to foster community and awareness through the literary arts. Our metaphor of organization purposefully looks backward toward the nineteenth century when Spartanburg was known as the "hub city," a place where railroads converged and departed.

As we approach the twenty-first century, Spartanburg is fast becoming the literary hub of South Carolina with an active and nationally celebrated core group of poets, fiction writers and essayists. We celebrate these writers—and the ones yet born—as one of our community's greatest assets. William R. Ferris, director of the Center for the Study of Southern Culture, says of the emerging South, "Our culture is our greatest resource. We can shape an economic base . . . And it won't be an investment that will disappear."

239

Holocene 1997

Not only the present geologic epoch, but a micropublisher in upstate South Carolina. We feature limited editions of poetry, broadsides, travel journals, and intelligent prose.

Cumberland Island Poems • John Lane (o.p.)	*The Questions of Postmodernism* • David Lehman
The Shuffle of Wings • Deno Trakas (o.p.)	*Weed Time* • John Lane
Poems for Che Guevara's Dream • Thomas Rain Crowe (o.p.)	*The Stars of Canaan* • Rucht Lilavivat
No Wrong Mountain • Ingrid Hutto (o.p.)	*Mistletoe* • John Lane (o.p.)
Yip-A Cowboy's Howl • David Romtvedt	*Juke Box Love* • Scott Gould
Usumacinta River Journey • John Lane, editor	*Vale of Academe* • Stephen Sandy
To See A World • John Harrington	*An Afternoon with K* • Jim Peterson
Poem for One Traveler • Martin Lammon (o.p.)	*Hub City Anthology* • John Lane & Betsy Teter, editors
Carvings on a Prayer Tree • Jim Peterson	*Hub City Music Makers* • Peter Cooper

(o.p.—Out of Print)

Colophon

Hub City Christmas was designed using a soon-to-be retired version of Adobe® Page-Maker® 5.0a on a "limping" Power Macintosh® 7100/80 packing semi-quad drives (totaling 4.3 gigs of possible storage, 1 gig unaccessable during this publication), 132 meg of ram, an indispensable HP ScanJet IIcx®, and the usual array of peripheral devices (excluding an Apple© mouse that had to be put to sleep) in a first edition of 4000 soft-bound and a limited edition of 150 case-bound copies. The display typefaces are Caslon Old Face and Lazy Dog Foundry's Glorietta. The body typefaces are members of Bitstream's Caslon 540 family. The small seasonal graphics are from the minds of PolyType and our good friends, Ron and Joe, at ArtParts. The book's designer and his nightly helpers utilized The Original Oldbury SHEEP DIP, the "Whisky Much Enjoyed by the Villagers of Oldbury-on-Severn."